PACESETTERS

# A FRESH START

HELEN OVBIAGELE

ISBN: 978-1-957076-83-6

NEO BOOKS

# Contents

# Chapter 1

Osifo woke up to the clatter of pots and pans as his next door neighbour, Mama Risi, set about her chores. She was a food-seller on one of the building sites in the Oke-Ofa area of Ibadan and she and her children woke up very early on weekdays to cook. He was used to the noise, and though he did not like it, he had to put up with it because there was no kitchen in the house. Tenants either cooked in their rooms or on the verandah outside their rooms.

He listened as Mama Risi issued orders to her children. 'Ramota, stir that soup and taste to see if there's enough salt. Bola, cover that eba with a tray before you start sweeping or sand will get in and customers will complain. I've told you so a dozen times. Where's Yemi? I suppose he's dozed off somewhere.'

No, Mama. I'm here attending to the rice. The water in it is dry now. Shall I take the pot off the fire?'

'Yes, but be careful, it's dark over there. Why don't you light a candle? Ade?'

'Ma?'

'Go and wake your father up, then put a pail of warm water in the bathroom for him. Bola, have you . . .?'

He stopped listening and looked at the clock by his bedside. A quarter past five. 'Gosh! I must get up and use the bathroom before the mad rush begins. He could hear doors opening as the other tenants woke up.

'Good morning, Mama Risi, He greeted her courteously when he went to fetch water from the tap.

'Good morning, Akowe,' replied Mama Risi. 'You're up early today. Are you all right?'

'Yes, Ma. I'm travelling home this morning so I have to leave for the motor park early.'

'Will you be away for long? Oh, it's holiday time, anyway.' 'Yes, it is. I shall leave the key of the ray room with you as usual for the landlord. I've already spoken to him about my journey.'

'All right, my son. Safe journey home. Choose a good vehicle with a sober driver. Too many drunken drivers these days.'

'That's true, Ma. Thank you,'

'I'll miss this place,' thought Osifo as he strapped up his bag. It was his last day in that house. He was not coming back for he was supposed to have completed his studies at St Francis Grammar School. Or so his family back home in Uzeri in Bendel State thought. But he had not. He had dropped out of school at the beginning of the first term in his fourth year, but had kept up the pretence of still being at school. So he duly went home on holiday, collected his school fees and came back to Ibadan.

He had not meant to drop out of school. It had just happened. He was sixteen and had just come back from the holidays. Boarders were requested to check in a few days before classes began. He had arrived on a Friday, feeling excited about his new class. He was a senior student now and had just two more years to go. Later that afternoon, he had gone to the market to make a few purchases. On his way back to school, close to the bus stop, he was attracted by a small crowd. He drew near. In the middle was a tall bearded man in a prophet's long white gown. He was addressing the crowd and making gestures in the air. From his accent Osifo could deduce he was from the neighbouring country of the Republic of Benin.

'See the wonders of God,' said the prophet in Yoruba. 'See your money doubled right under your nose. One naira becomes five naira. Five becomes ten. It's for believers only.'

One or two people jeered in the crowd. 'Ole, thief,' shouted one. Then a well-dressed man stepped forward. 'Look,' he said to the prophet, 'I believe in God. I trust you. Here's my five naira. Double it.'

The prophet took the money, put it in his pocket, and from another pocket he took a small stone, wrapped it up in a snow-white handkerchief and- handed it to the man. 'Now, put it in your pocket, shut your eyes, concentrate and say a short prayer. Good, now open your eyes and bring out the handkerchief.' The man unfolded the handkerchief and out fell a crisp ten naira note. Some people clapped, some gaped and some jeered.

'Thief!' 'Na lie.' 'Ole.'

A woman stepped forward and handed over a twenty naira note to the man. He doubled it. Two other people came forward. He repeated the process and doubled the money. Some people in the crowd began to argue about the man's authenticity.

'Na fake,' said one man. 'Na wayo, trick.'

'No be trick,' said one of those whose money had been doubled. 'The man na man of God, so God hear his prayer.'

'Why he no make himself rich?' challenged another. 'He no want,' said the believer, 'he no need the money. Na simple man.'

A woman with a baby tied to her back fingered the three twenty naira notes in her hand, then she stepped forward. Another person brought out fifty naira. The crowd was caught in the fever of money doubling. People pressed forward. It was then that Osifo, fascinated, handed over forty naira out of his school fees.

'With larger amounts, the money takes a longer time to double,' the prophet was saying as he handed out stones wrapped in white handkerchiefs here and there. The people were no longer listening. Heads were bent in prayer. The prophet quietly withdrew murmuring that he was tired. He then quickly disappeared around a corner. So also did his accomplices in the crowd.

Later, when it dawned on people that the stones would never turn into money, the atmosphere became charged. They began to look for the prophet, armed with bottles and sticks.

'Ah, ah, help me,' said the woman with a baby on her back, as she threw off her head tie and began to tear out her hair, sobbing. 'My God, oh my God. That was chop money for the month!'

'My husband will kill me today. He gave me that money to put in the bank,' wailed another woman.

'Well,' laughed the unbeliever, 'I told you he be fake. Thief! See now, he don cheat you and run away.'

'Shut up,' said one of those who had lost their money, 'or we go beat you up.'

'Ah, sorry O, my brother,' said the unbeliever and he quickly hurried away from the scene.

After looking in vain for the prophet the people trooped down to a nearby police station. There, a sergeant solemnly took down the description of the man, and said that the police would do their best to track him down as quickly as possible. His description would be relayed to all the police stations in Ibadan and environs, and motor parks and borders would be watched closely. He spoke so convincingly that the people were somewhat pacified and they dispersed moaning about their loss.

The sergeant did not think the man would ever be caught, but he knew what an irate mob was capable of. He did not want his station burnt down.

'Hmm! People will never learn!' he sighed to his companion after the people had left. 'You would think that with the large number of people who lose their money to money-doublers, the latter wouldn't get victims, but they do each time.'

Osifo had not followed the crowd to the police station. He had stood rooted to the ground, too stunned to believe he had really lost half of his school fees. He clutched the handkerchief in his hand.

A woman who sold cigarettes nearby and who had been watching him anxiously went over and laid a hand on his shoulder. 'My son, never mind what has happened. Go home and tell your parents. How much did you lose?'

He shook his shoulder free from her hand and walked away slowly. She sighed, shook her head and went back to her wares.

He got on a bus, his thoughts in chaos. What was he to do? He had been incredibly stupid. Usually, he was very careful with money. He never spent more than he could afford. He did not believe in money-doubling either, but the temptation that afternoon to make easy money had been too great. The man looked genuine too. After all, he was a holy man — a prophet. Perhaps now ... He unfolded the handkerchief. The stone was still there. What was he to do? Going back to Uzeri and telling his parents was out of the question as they were poor and could hardly afford his fees. Actually, he was the only child in the family who had been sent to a grammar school.

His two elder sisters and brother had had only a primary school education. He thought hard. Perhaps the Principal of his school would accept what was left of the fees while he did a part-time job. Then a thought occurred to him. He could become a day pupil. Yes! Saved! He calculated rapidly. Out of the fifty naira left, he would pay twenty naira for tuition, and with thirty naira look for accommodation.

His friends who were indigenes of Ibadan would know of a cheap place. He would work on weekends. Next term, things will be back to normal.

To reassure himself he felt in his pocket for his money. What was this? The money had disappeared! He remembered distinctly taking out forty naira from the ninety naira he had, and putting the rest back into the inner pocket of his trousers. Or didn't he? He panicked, got up and hit his head on the luggage rack of the bus. He felt all through his pockets. Nothing!

'Steady now, 'said the man next to him. 'Lost something?'

He collapsed into his seat, and burst into tears. Someone must have picked his pocket.

'Hey,' said the man behind him, 'What's the matter?'

'My money,' he wailed. 'It's gone. It was for my school fees. Oh my Lord!'

Most of the passengers were sympathetic, but some were not. The latter group fired questions at him. Where had he been? Why had he taken his fees to go shopping? It was a foolish thing to do. He should have handed the money over to a teacher on arrival. A big boy of his age should have had more sense than . .

He got down at his stop and walked the short distance to his college. He went straight to the dormitory and began to pack his things. The other students were playing on the field. He had made up his mind. He must leave school. There was nothing else to be done. He couldn't go home of course. He went to his house master's residence in the school compound and told him that, due to the sudden death of his father, he could no longer continue at school.

He had only come back to pack his things. Mr Olufemi, the house master, was sympathetic. Couldn't a relation help out? he asked. It would be a pity to end such a promising educational career. Couldn't he pay the first term's fees and then apply for a scholarship? Osifo shook his head sadly, explaining that he was the eldest child in the family and he had to take care of his mother and his younger brothers and sisters. The teacher then advised him that it was unsafe to travel that evening, and that he should spend the night in the dormitory.

When he took a bus to Oke-Ado the next morning, he had no clear plan in his mind. Where would he live? He went to Abe Street where his friend and classmate Wale Akanu lived with his parents. He was very surprised to see Osifo with his suitcase.

'What happened? Were you sent out of the dormitory?' Osifo explained that due to lack of funds he had withdrawn from school. He had come to leave his suitcase with Wale while he made future plans. Wale heaved a sigh of relief for he had thought that his friend had wanted accommodation. His parents never allowed him to have friends to stay over.

He liked Osifo very much and would have been sad not to be able to help him when he needed help.

'What are your plans? When are you going back home?'

I don't think I want to just yet. I thought I could pick up a job and then continue my studies in an evening school.'

'That's a good idea, but what type of job are you looking for?'

'Oh, anything will do since I've no formal training for anything.'

'Don't worry, Osifo,' soothed the other, 'something 'Will turn up. Do you need anything?' continued Wale. 'I've not been given my pocket money yet, but I could give you two naira.'

'Thank you, Wale. That would help. I will let you know when I'm fixed up. Meanwhile, please collect my mail at school and not a word of this to anyone. One day. I'll tell you what really took place. You wouldn't believe how stupid I've been.'

'Never mind. I'm sure things will be alright.'

'I hope so, too. Goodbye Wale. See you soon.'

'Goodbye,' he answered sadly as he watched his friend walk away. 'Hey Osifo, wait.' He ran after him. 'Don't follow anyone home. You've never actually lived among the people in this town. Strangers sometimes disappear. They are kidnapped, killed and their blood used to make medicine that will make others richer or live longer.'

'By whom?'

'Well, juju men. Anyone really. A friend can even sell you without your knowledge to a juju man. Don't trust anybody. I'm sure that sort of thing goes on in other parts of the country.'

'Yes, of course. Thanks, Wale. I'll be careful.'

'Where will you sleep tonight?' Wale asked anxiously.

'I . . . I . . . er . . . don't know. Yes, I do,' he lied, when he saw the look of alarm on his friend's face. 'I shall go to my mother's cousin in Bodija. I don't like him, but I can stay with him for a few days while I look for a job.'

'I would smuggle you into my room every evening but I share it with two other brothers and a cousin. Besides, my mother usually comes in to say goodnight.'

'That's okay. Thanks. I'll manage somehow.'

He picked up his little bag containing a few clothes and set off. He did not have enough money to rent a room. Perhaps he would get a live-in job. He spent the rest of the day calling various houses to ask if they needed a house-help. Yes, they did. But when he could not give references and a current address he was told he could not be employed for he might be a thief or something worse. He was very disappointed.

He knew exactly where to spend that night and subsequent nights until he got a place. A friend had once told him of a church where they held all night services. It was comparatively safe and members usually helped when you told them you were new in town and had nowhere to stay yet. You were allowed to sleep in one of the rooms provided you were sane and showed some interest in religion. From accompanying friends out, he knew Ibadan fairly well and knew where a church of this kind could be found.

As he made his way there later that evening he came across a street party. It was the usual pattern — the place was brightly lit up and chairs were arranged around tables on which were placed huge containers of food and drink. Special guests had reserved sections either inside the house or under gay canopies. Intruders, while not wholly welcome, were not sent away provided they stayed on the fringes and did not give any trouble whatsoever. They were served food and non-alcoholic drinks. Hosts considered it their own contribution towards helping to feed the poor and hungry.

The sight of all that food made Osifo realise how hungry he was. He sat down near a group of boys of about his own age, who were cracking silly jokes and eyeing the food greedily. Soon, a girl came round with a tray loaded with plates of jollof rice. Behind her, a boy carried a crate of soft drinks. Qsifo took a plate of food, murmured his thanks apd began to eat. He looked around. Most of the guests were gorgeously dressed — the women in particular. They were bedecked with gold. He watched, fascinated, as they moved about greeting friends and showing off their attire. It was the closest he had come to wealth.

A particular lady caught his attention. She was about thirty, tall and a little plump. She wore a Buba and Wrapper in blue and white lace with petals, a head tie in white and gold, and had black shoes and a handbag. She had not overdone her jewellery and she looked quite elegant. She did not get up to greet the other guests, instead, they greeted her courteously as they passed by her table. There was a young man on either side of her who fell over each other to fill her glass or bring her whatever she asked for. She didn't eat anything, and she took only the occasional sip from her glass.

Osifo's gaze kept wandering to her. He tried to imagine his mother dressed like that. He couldn't. Instead, he could see her hoeing on the farm; carrying a basket of yams or plantains; preparing food for the family, her eyes watering from the smoke of the firewood. And he could visualise his father, bent almost double from hard work on the farm. It was all because of him. They were wearing themselves out to send him to college so that he could lead a better life than they, and now he, who was supposed to bring home the golden fleece, had ruined everything. His eyes filled with tears.

One day, he promised himself, he would make it up to them.

Later that night, he was surprised when a girl brought him a plateful of fried meat and chicken. He hesitated then took a piece. 'It's for you,' said the girl, placing the plate in front of him. He noticed that no plate was placed in front of the other boys who were now openly eyeing him with envy. So he gestured to them and they fell on the meat without hesitation. When a boy brought him a bottle of beer, he declined it. He was puzzled. Why was he being singled out for such preferential treatment? Was it a mistake? He decided it was time to move on. He picked up his bag and had only taken a few steps when a man placed a hand on his shoulder. His heart froze as he whirled round.

'Madam Adunni would like to see you,' said the man, grinning. 'Come over here and wait for her.' Osifo found himself being led to a white Mercedes Benz.

'Who is Madam Adunni?' he protested. 'What have I done?'

'Easy, boy,' said the other. 'That's Madam Adunni over there,' and he pointed to the lady in the blue and white lace. She was smiling in their direction, and shortly she got up and went into the house to bid goodbye to the host and hostess of the party.

Osifo's fears about being kidnapped vanished as soon as he knew that the woman was involved. He couldn't explain it, but he trusted her somehow. He pushed aside Wale's warning. Anyway, he said to himself, he didn't really care what happened to him any more. Things couldn't be worse than they already were.

Madam Adunni walked over unhurriedly to where they stood, her two escorts on either side of her. 'Good evening, young man,' she greeted him, looking him over, 'I'm Madam Adunni. What's your name?'

'Good evening, Ma,' replied Osifo, his heart beating fast. The lady was indeed very pretty, and her perfume was overwhelming. It made him slightly dizzy. 'I'm Osifo Egie.'

'From Bendel State, isn't it? How old are you?' she asked, putting a hand on his shoulder.

'I'm eighteen, Ma,' he lied. Luckily, he was tall and looked much older than his age.

'Hmm, you look older than that. Fine. I need a driver for a new car I've just bought. Would you like to work for me?'

'But ... I ... I can't drive, madam,' he stammered. This was something he couldn't lie about. How did she guess he needed a job?

'Never mind,' she said smiling, 'Ade and Funsho here,' she pointed to her escorts, 'and even Papa Mulikat,' she pointed to the driver, 'can all drive. They'll teach you. You're not being forced into accepting the job, though. If you don't want to work for me . . .' She shrugged her lovely shoulders.

'Oh, I'd like to work for you, Ma,' said Osifo eagerly. 'I'll go home and tell my brother about the offer,' he lied. Although he didn't think he would come to any harm through the lady, he didn't want her or the others to know that he was alone and homeless in Ibadan. At the back of his mind was just the tiniest feeling of unease about going off with total strangers.

Madam Adunni looked at him and then at his bag. She didn't think there was a brother in Ibadan, but she said nothing. It suited her. She preferred boys without strong family ties. Anyway, her agents would carry out their own investigations if he came to work for her.

'That's fine,' she told him. 'Papa Mulikat and Ade will pick you up at this spot tomorrow evening between six and seven if you're here. Goodnight.'

'Goodnight, Ma. Thank you.'

They drove off and he went to spend the night in the church premises nearby. Madam Adunni's house stood in rambling grounds in a low population density area of Ibadan. It had all the marks of affluence. It consisted of a single storey building, a warehouse and an L-shaped bungalow where her workers lived. She lived with her mother in the main building.

There were no signs of a husband or children. Osifo could not tell exactly what the duties of the workers were. Papa Mulikat had warned him right from the onset that the fewer questions he asked, the less he knew, and that the less he knew, the better for him. He had stuck to that theory throughout his stay there. He noticed that every morning the workers, who numbered about ten, warmed up the cars, then they either went out or lazied around all day. By six however, everyone was back and at about eight he could hear the cars being driven off one after the other. Everywhere would become quiet until towards five in the morning when the cars were quietly driven in.

Although he had his own room where the others lived, he spent most of his time with Madam Adunni. He was not barred from going out and he went regularly to collect his mail from Wale, but he preferred to hang around most of the time so as to be near her. He had fallen in love with her, and it was not only out of gratitude to her for providing him with shelter. He truly adored her with all the intensity of a first love. Or so he thought. She, on the other hand, had only wanted to recruit him as one of her boys, but his good looks and polite manners had made her take him as a lover. He excited her and his dog-like devotion made her feel good.

Soon, he became her only escort to parties and she felt quite smug when her cronies cast envious glances in her direction. Why, even her best friend, Modinat, in whom she had confided how happy he made her, had once tried to lure him away.

She equipped his wardrobe with expensive clothes and taught him party manners. He learnt fast and in no time had become so full of confidence that she had to tell him jokingly to take it easy.

After living with Madam Adunni for two months, he lost all inclination to further his education. What was the point? He was in love, was well-cared for and was enjoying himself. He went to Uzeri when the schools were on holiday. His parents noticed nothing and suspected nothing. At the end of each term, he took a report home, and at the end of the academic year he promoted himself to the next class. It was easy. Wale bribed a junior clerk in the school secretary's office and was given several blank report sheets which Osifo filled in and presented to his father.

It was purely a formality, since his father only asked him whether he had passed or not and then kept the report which Osifo later destroyed.

One regular visitor to Madam Adunni's was a short middle-aged man with tribal marks. He was good-looking and was always well-dressed in a French suit or flowing Yoruba attire. As soon as he arrived, he would go to inspect the warehouse in the company of Madam Adunni or Papa Mulikat and then later retire to her apartment to discuss business. On these occasions Osifo would be told to make himself scarce. Not that he needed any persuasion, for he disliked this man who hardly ever acknowledged his greeting but instead looked past him as if he did not exist.

On enquiry, Ade told him that the man was known as 'Uncle Abiodun'; he then advised Osifo not to ask any more questions about him. Of all his colleagues, he liked Ade and Papa Mulikat most. They talked to him and made him feel at home, whereas conversations usually stopped when he stepped into the room where the others were and that made him feel unwanted.

One evening, Ade had left with the others and Osifo never saw him again. When he asked Papa Mulikat what had happened, the latter had shaken his head and had turned away. 'Adunni,' said Uncle Abiodun one day when they were alone in her apartment, 'I must congratulate you on your latest acquisition.'

'What? Oh, you mean Osifo? He's a darling. He's so sweet.'

'Hm, he's not bad-looking, at least. Which could not be said of his predecessor who was one of nature's eyesores.'

'Osifo is gorgeous,' she gushed. 'Quite innocent he was at the beginning, but my, can he learn fast!'

'Learn what fast? He looks quite stupid to me. Funsho told me he neither drinks alcohol nor smokes. In fact, I understand he almost passed out the first time weed was smoked in his presence.

He'd be useless in an operation. Lacks guts. Where did you pick him up?'

'At Shade's party. However, I did not engage him for operations.'

'What's he here for then?'

'That's my business. He pleases me. He worships me, he's so gentle and I suspect he's in love with me.'

'Ha, ha! Nonsense! I guess he's just after your money. The bastard is probably a thief. You'll wake up one morning to find all your jewellery gone.'

'I doubt it. He's passed my tests. He's not after my money. Besides, I was told he dropped out of St Francis Grammar School because of lack of finance. So, you see, his background is fine.'

'Oho!' laughed Abiodun heartily, slapping his knee. 'So, you now harbour truants. Ha, ha!'

'None of your business,' said Adunni heatedly. 'The boy is good for me. He makes me feel young and beautiful.'

'You're always beautiful, Adunni,' he said seriously. 'Chuck this boy out and stop this cradle-snatching game. After all, you always get fed up with these boys later. Come back to me. You know I love you still.'

'Don't be ridiculous, Abiodun. Let's stick to being business partners. Our relationship works better that way. We were married for ten years then you left me for a younger woman. Now you want me back. What for? I wonder what place you have for me among your other three wives.'

'You can continue to live here . . .'

'Please, no more. Leave me alone.'

Osifo's relationship with Madam Adunni lasted exactly eleven months, after which she got tired of him and told him to leave. He was completely shattered. His nice safe life was over and his very first love had rejected him. He knelt in front of her and, with tears in his eyes, pleaded to be allowed to stay near her in any capacity. She laughed and told him not to be silly. Did he think that she had adopted him and that he was going to live with her forever?

In the end he was given two hundred naira and Papa Mulikat was told to go and drop him at a motor park. Papa Mulikat, who was secretly sorry for the naive boy, took him to a landlord in Oke-Ofa who he knew had vacant rooms. He advised Osifo to pay about nine months' rent in advance from the money so that he could at least be sure of accommodation for that period while he looked for something to do. This he did.

He couldn't go back to grammar school because he had missed out a year and many schools were reluctant to accept dropouts of his age and height. He enrolled at an evening school and got a job in a soft drinks factory, but he could not cope.

The strain of lifting and loading during the day, and studying during the night, was too much for him and after a few months his health broke down and he had to give up work to concentrate on his studies. These he had to abandon too when he could not pass his examinations.

However, it was now two years since he had left school; his classmates had sat for the final examinations for the West African School Certificate and finally left school. Osifo could no longer pretend he was still at school so he had to go back home too.

# Chapter 2

He alighted from the lorry at the village motor park and waited patiently for the 'motor boy' to bring down the passengers' luggage from the rack on top of the lorry. He looked around him. It was two in the afternoon and the place was bustling with activity as usual. Actually, the motor park was the nerve-centre of any village. On one side of it was a long row of 'bukas' where people ate. On the other side, lorries and 504 taxi cabs queued up for passengers. Touts were everywhere trying to get passengers for them.

'Dis way, dis way for Benin City,' shouted one man.

'One more passenger for Agbor. We don ready to go,' yelled another.

'Lef me, I say lef me,' cried a woman angrily as she was being urged by two touts to get into their vehicles.

'Come now,' said one of them persuasively. 'Dis driver na careful wan. Come.'

'Lef me,' the woman cried again, shaking herself free. 'Dat your driver wey dey drive like craze man! I don follow am before. His lorry no get brakes. I no wan die yet.' She hissed at him and walked away.

'Yeye woman,' called the tout after her, 'you no get money for travel sef.' Then he dashed off for another prospective passenger.

'Oga, orange,' called a little girl at Osifo's elbow. 'Two for five kobo. E sweet. Make I peel am?'

He bought two and began to eat them thoughtfully. What was he going to tell his parents? Make a clean breast of everything and ask for forgiveness or continue with the deception and pretend that he was actually awaiting his examination results? What would he do later? Perhaps he would leave Uzeri and try to make a future for himself somewhere.

Everywhere was quiet as he walked along the only main road which led to the village. Most of the people had gone to their farms and only the aged and the very young were at home. As he came to the dwelling houses, children ran to him yelling at the top of their voices.

'Welcome home, brother Osifo;' they cried. 'Did you bring us some sweets?' They tugged at his sleeves. He did not disappoint them. He smiled indulgently as he shared the sweets.

'Oh, thank you, brother Osifo,' said one boy.

'Here, let me help you with your box,' offered another.

'No, I will carry it,' said yet another.

'No, I will carry it.'

'No, I will! It's too heavy for you.'

'It isn't! You only want to earn yourself some extra sweets.' They began to fight,

'Okay, okay,' said Osifo. 'I will carry it myself. Thank you. Now be off, both of you.'

The village blacksmith, shopkeeper and carpenter all came out to greet him, congratulating him on the completion of his studies and urging him to get a good job in one of the big cities and come back to help develop Uzeri.

His mother was breaking up firewood at the back of the house when she caught sight of him. She flung down the axe and rushed at him and threw herself into his arms.

'Osifo' Osifo, my son! ' she cried. 'Welcome home. Today is one of the happiest days in my life. My son has completed his studies at last. No-one, absolutely no-one can mock your father and me any more.

All these years we've been the butt of jokes in the village because none of our children had been educated beyond Primary Six. And when we sent you to college, people jeered. They believed we couldn't keep you there, but your father and I struggled, and now all my enemies have been put to shame. Yes, to shame! You have completed your studies now and I can walk about with my head held high.' She hopped a bit and danced a few steps. Then she turned to the direction of the river and raised her arms to the sun. 'Olokun, the goddess of water, I thank you O! I thank you for seeing my son, who is also your son, through his studies, and for bringing him home safely to me.

For that, I'll make a sacrifice of the Whitest and fattest fowl of my poultry to you. I will give you a big goat if he gets a good job with good pay, so that from now on, my husband and I will lead a more comfortable life. It is time we retired from our poverty. I thank you O, Olokun. Don't let me down. Come, come, my son,' she said to Osifo, 'Your father is waiting for you. He has a visitor. An important man from Benin City.'

Osifo caught a glimpse of a driver at the wheel of a cream coloured Range Rover. They rarely had visitors with cars and he wondered who the man was. He picked up his suitcase, and with a heavy heart followed his mother into the house. How he wished things were different.

He went to the parlour where his father and the visitor were and bowed low to greet them.

'Ah, there you are, Osifo my boy,' said his father, laughing heartily. 'Welcome back home! I can hear your mother shouting at the back of the house. I'm sure she's telling all and sundry of the return of her son. Hm, that woman! Talk, talk, talk! At her age.' Both men laughed.

'Ugo,' he said, turning to the man, 'let me introduce my son Osifo. He's the last-bom. You've met him once, I think, when he was a baby. You had just returned from England and you came to invite me to the burial ceremonies of your father.'

'Yes, I remember now. Hello, young man. The baby of yesterday is now a man.'

'He's just completed his studies at St Francis Grammar School, in Ibadan.'

'Is that so? What are your plans?' asked Chief Amengo, taking a piece of kolanut and a grain of alligator pepper from a saucer by his side. He was a huge man with a booming voice and he was dressed in immaculate white agbada with a red and gold embroidered cap, and white leather shoes. He had an ebony walking stick. His impressive appearance made everything else in the room very ordinary.

Osifo was surprised to hear his father say that they had been classmates in a primary school in Agbor for the man looked considerably younger than his father, who he had thought was in his sixties. The men must be in their mid-fifties. It must be the hard work on the farm that made his father look so old.

'Erm I don't know yet, sir. My father will have to decide what I should do.'

'Why don't you go for further studies if your results are good? There are so many avenues open now for you young people. There are the universities, the colleges of education, the technical colleges and the polytechnics and so many courses to choose from. Tuition is free. My friend here can manage and . .

       'No, I think he should work for a while and then go for further studies later on. The experience will do him some good and also bring us some financial relief. He's a bright boy and he's still young. There's no hurry.'

'Yes, but the earlier he goes for these studies the better. It may be rough for you now, but later things would be fine when he qualified. Think about it.'

'All right, I will.'

'It all depends on his results. Look, Osifo, come and see me when your results are out. I'll see what I can do for you. Here's my card.'

'Oh, thank you, sir. Thank you.'

'Yes, there's nothing like a good education,' said Mr Egie. 'Look at you, Ugo. A prominent lawyer turned politician. If I had paid more attention to my studies in those days instead of thinking that hard work on the farm was all that mattered, things would be different today.'

'But farmers are important and there are rich ones.'

'Yes, but not our type. We always have poor yields.'

Chief Amengo refrained from telling his friend that he had remained poor because he had not been adventurous enough to experiment in modern farming. Mr Egie shunned fertilisers and the like and stuck to the old method which was back-breaking and frustrating, particularly now that the same soil had to be farmed over and over again due to shortage of land. He also refused to take a bank loan for expansion despite government propaganda about easy-term loans for farmers. Debts of any sort scared him, he claimed.

'Well, I must be on my way. I still have to call on some people here before I go back. Emma, you won't forget what we discussed, will you? You'll help me with my campaign? The people here do not like my party, but you're quite popular with the elders. I'm relying on you to use your influence to help get us some votes.'

'I've told you I don't want to get involved in politics.'

'Why not? As a responsible adult, Emma, you should be interested in the running of your country. My party is the best. It is the only one that can save the country from imperialism, feudalism and all the other 'isms' that are bad. Ha! Ha!'

'Hm! Ugo, you and your big words!'

Three months soon sped by and the results for the West African School Certificate examinations were out. Some schools had theirs published in the papers. Mr Egie became particularly anxious when Fred, the shopkeeper's son, came to announce to Osifo that he had passed in Grade 1.

He brought along his result sheet. Osifo had grown lean and gaunt. His father could not understand why he had not heard from his school. After all, there had been no rumours about an examination leakage there. He decided that Osifo should travel to Benin City to see Chief Amengo who had a son who worked for the West African Examination Council, the examining body.

It was at this stage that Osifo threw himself on the ground and confessed to his father that he had dropped out of school two and a half years before. He omitted the details about Madam Adunni.

His father was stunned. He sat for a long while in silence. It was the deception that hurt most. His own son, coming home on holiday, collecting money for his school fees and then going back to ibadan to lead an idle life while he and his wife worked their fingers to me bone to get enough money to keep body and soul together. There was no help from any other source. His eldest son, Ifeanyi, was a struggling trader and his two married daughters who lived in Asaba with their families had their own responsibilities.

He gave a bitter laugh. To think that any child of his would be stupid enough to believe in money- doublers! What his grandmother used to say was, that 'It is the son of the poor man who is foolish with money,' Could it be a sort of punishment from God for something he or his wife had done wrong? He looked at his son who was still Kneeling in front of him, with his head bowed. The boy looked so miserable that he found it difficult to get angry with him.

What agony he must have been through all these months! Besides, he had been a loving and obedient child in the past and had not given the family any anxiety.

'Get up, Osifo, I'm prepared to forgive what you've done. I cannot pretend that I'm not deeply hurt and disappointed, but what has happened has happened. You're forgiven, but you must promise that you will always tell the truth, no matter how bitter, in things that matter.'

'Thank you. Papa, I promise,' he said.

'Now, not a word of this to your mother. She wouldn't understand what had happened. We'll have to think carefully now of your future. What do you think you're capable of doing? You're eighteen and must have some idea of what you'd like to do.'

'I would very much like to finish my interrupted education. Papa. Make a fresh start, but at the same time, I realise that you and Mama are not getting any younger, so I think I will work first and study later.'

'Well, if . . .'

'Don't worry, Papa, I think you've made enough sacrifices for me already. Let me try to find my own feet. I know now how foolish I have been, but I've suffered too. You cannot imagine the agony I went through while deceiving you both.'

'Oh, my son. Well, never mind, so long as you're quite sure you've learnt your lesson, things will work out fine.'

'I have, Papa.'

'We'll have to enlist the help of Chief Amengo. He's an influential man in Bendel State and he'll have no difficulty in getting you a job. The only snag is that Till now I have to help him with that damned campaign of his. His party is not popular here. Neither is he, for he has done nothing to develop this area.'

'But he's not from our village, Papa.'

'Yes, but he has a family house here. His father was the catechist here for a long time and he spent most of his childhood here. Ute, his village, is only about fifty kilometres from Uzeri, and what has he done there? Nothing! They have no electricity and no pipe-borne water like us. For years he neglected this area and has only just begun visiting frequently because he wants votes. I was told that he's rebuilding his crumbling family house. He's selfish and a snob. He has over twelve lovely houses in Benin City, Agbor, Onitsha and Lagos, yet his children have never been to his village. The only good thing he has done was to establish a palm produce processing factory in Ute, and this was at my insistence, when he told me a few years ago that he was going into politics.

There's high unemployment here and most of our young men leave for the cities to seek their fortune, but once there, they forget all about developing their villages. The good ones visit once in a while or send money to their families. It is sad. The siting of industries here will partially help to stem the outflow of these young people. However, I'll do my best to help Chief Amengo.'

'If you really don't want to help him. Papa, don't. I'll get a job somehow. I could go to Ifeanyi in Agbor or my sisters in Asaba. I'll get fixed up.'

'No, go to Chief Amengo. He's in a better position to help you.'

Although thrilled at the prospects of going to see a 'big man' about a job, Osifo was a bit apprehensive about having to tell him that he had failed his examinations, as his father had told him to.

He went past Chief Amengo's house several times before he plucked up the courage to go in. He went to the section marked 'Chambers' where a receptionist told him to wait while she announced him. He was then shown into a very large room where about ten people, mostly men, were waiting at one end. The Chief was sitting at a large table at the other end and was listening with rapt attention to the man in front of him. He waved Osifo to a chair.

'Nice to see you again, Osifo,' he boomed. 'Please take a seat. How are your parents? How did you fare in your examinations?' Osifo mumbled something non-committal in reply,

'I'll see you in a minute. These are people from my constituency who have come to see me about one problem or the other,' he said smiling expansively. 'As a politician, I'm a servant to all.' Some of the people shuffled their feet and smiled.

Osifo looked around the room. It had a wall-to- wall grey carpet and deep armchairs. A large refrigerator stood in a comer and two air-conditioners hummed away. The place was comfortable but was in no way as posh as Madam Adunni's office. From their clothes he could tell that most of the people were labourers or farmers. He could recognise two from his village. They looked tense and worried. Some had come to see Chief Amengo about jobs, others about cases pending in the courts. They waited patiently.

Chief Amengo devoted Friday afternoon and the greater part of Saturday to seeing people from his constituency. Of course, he had not always been as genial as this. He was a self-made man who had worked hard all his life, and having established himself as a well-known lawyer and businessman, his dearest wish now was to be elected a member of the National House of Assembly. It would be good for business and prestige. He had been an active member of the Common Man's Party of Nigeria for several years and he contributed huge sums of money to party funds. He did not, however, make the plight of the common man his business, as borne out by the fact that his workers were amongst the lowest paid in the country.

'Resign if you like,' he would tell his discontented staff, who were not allowed to form a union. 'The government didn't set up this factory for me, so they cannot tell me what to pay you,' he added when someone pointed out that their wages were below the minimum recommended by the Federal Government. At the moment, however, he was trying to be nice to everyone.

At last it was Osifo's turn to see the Chief.

'Ah, here you are at last,' he said amiably. 'I'm sorry it took so long. Now, what can I do for you?'

'Er ... I'm sorry to bother you, sir. My father said I should see you about a job.'

'Ah, you've decided to work first before going for further studies?'

'Yes sir.'

'What can you do?'

'Er . . . I really cannot say, sir, but I'll try anything.'

'Well, I have a place for an Assistant Supervisor in my factory in Ute. Would you like such a job?

'Oh, yes sir! I'll try it.

'You wouldn't mind living in a small village?*

'I don't think so.'

'Good, that's settled. But I demand hard work, and,' here he lowered his voice, 'while there, you'll be my eyes and ears. I don't trust the Supervisor, but I can't sack him. At least not yet. You see, he's my wife's brother. He's lazy and is a big cheat. And now, about salary.' Here, he raised his voice for the benefit of the others in the room. 'I'll pay you the recommended minimum wage of one hundred and twenty-five naira.'

Elsewhere, the post would attract a monthly salary of at least one hundred and fifty naira with some fringe benefits thrown in, but still, some of the people in the room looked at Osifo with envy as they felt he was too young to be given such salary. The Chief noticed this and quickly added, 'Well, that's because you've been to college and are a School Certificate holder. What was your grade?'

'Er ... I was coming to that, sir,' Osifo said as he broke out in perspiration in the cool room, 'As a matter of fact I er . . . er . . . '

'Not that it matters,' continued the Chief, who was looking at his watch and wondering if he could still see some people that day before leaving for a political rally at Etina. 'You must spend the night with us, Osifo. Go and wait in the next room. I'll ask someone to take you to my wife.'

'Thank you, sir.'

At the door, a girl of about sixteen pushed roughly past him into the room. She was light in complexion, slim and long-legged. She had long woven hair with red beads in it and wore a pair of tight slacks and a T-shirt. Osifo stopped briefly to look at her, surprised that she had not apologised for almost knocking him down. 'Popsie, Popsie,' cried the girl, rushing to Chief Amengo, 'could I go to the disco session at La Belle this afternoon?'

'Ah, hello, Ndidi,' the Chief greeted her fondly. 'Those feet of yours must have wings. You almost knocked my visitor over. Osifo,' he called, raising his voice. Osifo came back into the room. 'Meet my daughter, Ndidi. She's just left St Monica's College, Jos, and will be going to Britain shortly to do her 'A' levels. Ndidi, this is Osifo Egie, the son of my good friend in Uzeri. He's going to be the Assistant Supervisor in Ute.'

'Hello, Ndidi,' said Osifo.

'Hello,' said Ndidi, hardly giving him a glance. 'Popsie, may I go to this disco? Esohe and May are going too.'

'Disco? At La Belle? Eh, let me see now. You can go, but make sure you're back by nine o'clock. I may not be home then and I don't want you to give your mother any anxiety by coming home late.'

'Oh, thank you, Popsie,' she said effusively. 'I shall be home by ten-thirty.'

'Nine.'

'Isn't that a bit early? They may not start on the dot of four. The D.J. might be late, the equipment might break down . . .'

'Nine o'clock, Ndidi, or you stay at home.'

'Oh all right, nine then.' She turned to go.

'Eh, Osifo will accompany you.'

'What!' she exclaimed, whirling round. 'Who will accompany me? Him? I don't know him.' She looked at Osifo as if he were a horrible insect.

'Well, you do now. He'll go with you.'

'But why, Popsie? Can't I look after myself? I've been to discos on my own before.'

'Sure. But, you see, Osifo is our guest for the night, so we'll have to entertain him. As a teenager like yourself. I'm certain he'll enjoy going to the disco.'

'If you don't mind, sir,' said Osifo, 'I'd rather stay behind and watch the television. I'm not keen on dancing.' He loved dancing, but knew when he was not wanted.

'That doesn't matter,' said Chief Amengo. 'You can watch others dance and still have a nice time. You'll be lonesome here all on your own. My sons are all away and my wife likes to retire to her room after supper.'

He was not worried at all about Osifo being bored, rather, he thought that his presence at La Belle would help check whatever excesses Ndidi might want to indulge in. He knew she was sensible but he believed it was very easy for young girls to fall into bad company if they went by themselves to such places.

Things had been much easier when his sons were around and took it in turns to take her to parties. If he had his way, discos would be banned and teenage girls kept under lock and key until they had finished their studies and could fend for themselves. He was keeping his fingers crossed that things would go well with Ndidi in Britain.

Osifo felt out of place at the disco. Everybody knew everyone else and people gathered in groups chatting or dancing. It was difficult to break in and join any group without an introduction. Ndidi had not said a word to him since they left home, and when they got there she had joined a group of her friends and left him to his own devices.

He bought a drink and stood around sipping it. The music was good and he would have liked to dance but did not fancy dancing without a partner. He wondered what Ndidi would say if he asked her for a dance. Something insolent, no doubt. He decided not to risk it. Some of her friends looked at him with interest and then whispered to her. She looked carelessly in his direction and laughed. He felt embarrassed, took his drink into the fruit machine room and stayed there for the rest of the evening. He wished he had had the courage to refuse bluntly to accompany her. She made him feel like an inferior being.

Ndidi did not mean to be unkind, but she resented Osifo's company being forced on her. Who was he anyway? A nonentity from Uzeri! A prospective clerk! He was not bad looking, but how would she introduce him to her friends? Now, if he had been the son of a judge like Tunde Obasohan, or Ivan Soho, the popular D.J. at La Belle who was also a newscaster on the television, it would have been a different matter. These were the two men of her dreams at the moment. Unfortunately, other girls were interested in them too and she was just a face in the crowd.

Osifo was staring angrily at the machine that had swallowed up his two naira and was about to give it another kick when Ndidi came to tell him it was time to go home. She looked unhappy.

'Did you enjoy yourself?' he asked in the taxi on the way. She mumbled something and turned her face away. The evening had been disappointing for her. Tunde had turned up with a girl who had stuck to him like a leech all evening and Ivan had not looked even once in her direction despite the fact that she had joined the group of girls who had surrounded him, and had talked louder than anyone else.

A week later, Osifo started his new job. Chief Amengo had taken him down to Ute in his car and had watched with delight the look of murder on the Supervisor's face when he was presented with an assistant out of the blue. Osifo was given a room in the staff quarters near the factory and he tried as hard as he could to settle down. It was not easy. Mr Atalo, the Supervisor, did not want an assistant, and he decided that he would make the job so unbearable for the young man that he would leave of his own volition. He therefore spread the news around that Osifo was the Chief's spy, so most of the workers were hostile to the boy right from the start.

Stealing was a widespread practice in the factory, and there was hardly any camouflage. Tins of palm oil and coconut oil were openly carried away by the workers, and their families. Sometimes a daring one would even invite his customers to come and buy from him at the factory. The Supervisor never stole any of the products and he was usually elsewhere while his workers did, but at the end of each week he was given a fixed sum of money by each worker. He recorded only three-quarters, and sometimes only half of the daily production. Full of zeal and enthusiasm, Osifo reported these goings- on to the Chief who severely reprimanded the Supervisor and sacked several workers.

Some of the latter, who felt that Osifo was responsible for the loss of their jobs, made complaints to his father, who apologised to them and gave them gifts to produce from his farm. Others were not so kind. They waylaid him on his way to the village and he was severely beaten. The other workers declared total hostility towards him — they carried out his instructions concerning their jobs but no-one spoke to him. When snakes began to appear in all the nooks and corners of his room he moved out of the staff quarters to live with his brother Ifeanyi in Agbor and commuted to work on the latter's battered bicycle.

Sensing how acutely unhappy his son was at Ute, Mr Egie invited all the workers to lunch one weekend. Most of them came because he was liked and respected in the area. After lunch, he publicly apologised for his son's over-zealousness in the performance of his duties; this he attributed to youthful exuberance.

Mellowed by the food and drink, and Mr Egie's eloquence, many of them got up to embrace the boy and tell him that all was forgiven. From thenceforth his relationship with them improved, but he had had enough. While not condoning the thefts that went on, he sympathised, however, with the workers, and deplored Chief Amengo's lack of concern for his workers' welfare. He developed a strong dislike for him. The Chief was only kind to people when he knew he was going to get a favour in return, and as soon as they had served his purpose, he had no more time for them.

Osifo did not see a future in his job. After two years he was still on the same salary and the Chief was not willing to help him to get a better position. So, he decided he would have to make a move on his own, and with the one hundred and eighty naira he had saved, he left for Ibadan.

# Chapter 3

Osifo's first place of call when he got to Ibadan was his friend Wale's. Somehow during the last two years their correspondence had petered out. He was told Wale was a second year Economics student at the University of Ibadan, and was residing on the campus. He felt remorse at his own interrupted educational career. Would Wale want to see him now? He needn't have worried. Wale was as glad to see him as ever.

'Hello, Osifo,' he exclaimed on entering the students' common-room of his Hall. 'This is a great surprise!' Osifo jumped to his feet and they embraced.

'Hello, Wale,' he said, slapping his friend on the back. 'Here, let me look at you. How slim and tall you've become.'

'Oh, not as tall as you are. You must be at least six feet tall now and you're looking very well and handsome too. Come, let's go up to my room. You must tell me all you've been doing.'

In Wale's room, the boys talked non-stop for almost an hour, mostly about old classmates. Osifo narrated all that had happened to him since they had last communicated and Wale was sorry to hear that his friend still had no settled plans for the future. He was eager to help him but did not know what advice he could give. He thought hard for some minutes,

'Look, Osifo, wait here. Pm going to get a friend of mine who's given me some very useful advice in the past. He's much older than me although we are both in the same class. He's seen a lot of life and he likes organising people. His name is Dipo Mwanga. Don't be put off by his appearance. He looks like a prize-fighter and he clowns most of the time but deep down he has a serious disposition and a responsible attitude towards life, and is quite kind. He said he used to be a bodyguard to one of our leading politicians.'

'Really? He sounds interesting. I would very much like to meet him.'

Wale soon came back with the man. Dipo really looked like a thug. He was short, thickset and heavily bearded. He had on a black shirt over a pair of white trousers, a black beret, wore one earring and a pair of very dark glasses. His left hand was covered with evil-looking rings.

'Osifo, this is Dipo, a very good friend of mine.'

'Hiya, Osifo,' said Dipo, stretching out his hand. 'Here, shake paws. I like your face. Now what can I do to help you? I'm a very busy man. I am Atlas and I have the whole world on my shoulders, but I can still spare some minutes.'

'Please, Dipo,' begged Wale laughing, 'quit clowning for a minute and listen. There isn't much to tell. We just need advice.'

'All right, shoot.'

Briefly, he was told about Osifo's interrupted educational career. He adjusted his glasses and looked sternly over their rims at Osifo.

'Dropped out! Dropped out of school! He repeated, moving his face close to Osifo's, who turned to Wale, helplessly embarrassed. 'Now why did you do such a silly thing? Don't you know knowledge is beautiful and that he who willingly refuses to acquire it shall be cast into utter darkness where there's wailing and gnashing of teeth, and dragons?'

'Please be serious, Dipo,' pleaded Wale once again.

'Hush! I'm thinking. Don't interrupt. Clowning helps the brain to relax. Now I've got it. Your friend must obtain his 'O' levels. This will form his basic qualification, and from there he can do other things.

' 'O'levels!' exclaimed Osifo. 'How? I've not been near any form of book for almost five years. I doubt if I can concentrate now. I'm too old for 'O' levels. '

'Too old! Well, that's your business. Laziness, if you ask me. Wale, does your friend here want to be helped or is he going to raise objections to sensible suggestions?'

'Osifo, listen to what Dipo has to say.'

'I'm sorry. Please carry on,' said Osifo, ashamed of himself.

'Apology accepted. Now, I know of a good evening school in Dugbe which is run by a man from my village. I think his fees are high, but I was told he has good teachers and the percentage of passes each year is fair.'

'How long do you think it will take me to pass five or six papers?'

'That depends on how hard you work. It could take you all your life or just one year. However, this shylock friend of mine also runs a hostel for young men just a stone's throw from his school, for which he charges ten naira a month excluding meals. So, there you are! Some of your problems are solved.'

'Great! Thank you very much, Dipo. If you give me your friend's address. I'll go and see him right away.'

'As for money,' put in Wale, 'I can only help with thirty naira. Perhaps later . . .'

'Oh, no, no! I can't possibly accept. After all, you're a struggling student yourself. I've got something to get on with for the meantime. Thanks all the same.'

'I was coming to the question of money. There's a lot of it around but mostly in the wrong pockets. However, you could work for my friend. His pay is so poor that he's constantly short of workers. I'd be surprised if he has no vacancy at the hostel now.

The last time I saw him he was looking for a caretaker for the place. If the offer is still open, it might suit you. You'd have a room on the premises. You can refuse the offer if it doesn't suit you. Here, I'll give you a note for him.'

'Thank you, Dipo.'

'A thousand thanks, Dipo, old fellow,' added Wale. 'I knew we could rely on you.'

'I'm glad to have been of help, but I must say that your friend needs a lot of pushing. He should be more daring at his age and get rid of his reluctance to take on a challenge. Don't ever mention his name to me again if he fails to make five or six papers within a year. I like success. Good day.'

That parting shot of Dipo's was what kept Osifo at his studies during the next twelve months and later on. Combining the duties of a caretaker at the hostel with his studies was not at all easy and, as usual when things were not going smoothly, he wanted to give up but this time he persevered. After all, it was his life. If he wanted a good and a secure future, he would have to work hard. He passed five out of the eight papers he sat for and he applied for a place to do Electronics Engineering at the Federal Polytechnic in Makurdi. Dipo wanted him to try for 'A' levels and, if successful, gain a direct entry into one of the universities, but he wasn't keen.

'What do you want to study at the Polytechnic then?' asked Dipo one day when he called to see him at the hostel.

'Horology.'

'Horo, what?' asked the other, stupefied.

'Horology. Watch or clock making.'

'I know what horology is. What I mean is, why would a he-man like you go messing about with watches and clocks. I thought it was a job for the effeminate.'

'No, it isn't,' laughed Osifo. 'It is a special art. Frankly, clocks have always fascinated me and I was delighted when I heard that this course was being offered at Makurdi. '

'Yes, but you can't make much money from it afterwards. '

'Oh yes, you can. Lots. Don't think of watch repairs as carried out by the man who sets up his workshop by the roadside. Think of industries that manufacture safes, alarms, clocks, wrist-watches and a whole range of articles in that line.'

'Yes, I understand.'

'Apart from the money, which I'm not so crazy about, I want to do something I actually enjoy doing. It's a chance I don't want to miss.'

'Hmm, a profession that involves listening to things tick would send me up the wall. Still, it's your life. Good luck, pal.'

'Thanks.'

On the successful completion of the course which lasted three years, Wale and Dipo, who were now working in Lagos, tried to persuade Osifo to come and work there too. 'Lagos is where all the action is,' Wale told him. He declined, saying he couldn't cope with the pace of life there. He had a soft spot for Ibadan so he got a job with a Chinese electronics company there and lived in a two-bedroomed flat in Oke-Ado. Although his pay wasn't high, he liked his position of Assistant Engineer in the company and he tried as much as possible to establish a foothold in his profession. The indigenisation decree demanded that there be a gradual transfer of technology to Nigerians, so various courses were organised by companies for their employees. After attending two such courses he was promoted to the post of Engineer.

He was very pleased at the progress he had made. His parents were thrilled and a big party was organised for him in Uzeri. He was told to come with some of his friends, and he went down with Wale and Dipo. Wale felt a bit awkward for he had never been to a village in Bendel State before, but Dipo was in his element.

He had travelled all over Nigeria during his days as a party thug and anywhere was home to him. He was the life and soul of the party as he drank and ate whatever was placed before him and danced jigs with almost all the village damsels. People warmed to him and he rose to make speeches several times in pidgin English, Yoruba, Hausa and Igbo. For months after the party, the villagers still talked about him, and Mr Egie was constantly asked when Osifo was going to bring down his funny friend again.

Osifo found life even more pleasant when he bought his car. He was able to drive to places that held special memories for him: where he used to live at Oke-Ofa; where he lost his school fees to a money-doubler ('One day I'll bring my children to this spot,' he promised himself); and Madam Adunni's house. He drove past it several times trying to catch a glimpse of any of the old faces, but he did not stop and go into the house. 'What would I say to her?' he thought. He had not seen her since he was thrown out almost eleven years before. Has she aged? Was she still living the same life-style? There was no-one to ask.

One day, he was at a house-warming party given by Mr Are, the Financial Director of the company when in came Madam Adunni with a young man of about twenty-two. Osifo almost passed out at this sudden apparition from his past. She walked past him and even looked at him but did not appear to recognise him.

He looked at her closely. She had aged slightly and was a little bit slimmer, but she was as lovely as ever, and had dressed with her usual good taste. She walked with her habitual unhurried steps, flashing her lovely smile as she acknowledged greetings here and there. Her nervous escort hovered by her side. Mr Are and his wife hurried out to meet her and lead her to the section reserved for special guests. There was no doubt that she was still held in high esteem in the social circles of Ibadan. It must be the money. He looked at her and thought of their days together. A lump came into his throat.

Later that night when the floor was packed full with dancers, he plucked up enough courage to go and ask her for a dance. He half expected her to refuse, but she didn't. She looked at him and frowned when he bowed to her, but she got up all the same. He held her close as they danced, excitedly coursing through him. After a while she stopped dancing, drew back from him and took a good look at him. 'I remember you now,' she said, her eyes narrowing. 'You're Osifo.'

'Yes, madam,' he admitted, bowing to her and attempting a smile. She said nothing more. She left him on the dance floor and walked away. He was perplexed. He tried to go after her but was delayed by other dancers who were wriggling away all around him. When he finally got to where she had sat he found that she had collected her things and had left. He never saw her again.

He had been working for his company for about six years when the outgoing General Manager, Mr Wang, called him into his office one day to ask him what his future plans were. He was surprised and he wondered what the other man had in his mind. Was he going to be fired? The company might not be the most generous one around but he did enjoy working there and had no immediate long-term plans.

'Er, what exactly do you mean by future plans, Mr Wang?'

'You might think I'm intruding, but I wanted to find out if you would be interested in setting up a business of your own in future.'

'I can't sincerely say I've given it much thought.'

'Well, as you know. I'm leaving this country soon to go back home to Hong Kong. Actually, I've resigned from this company. My two brothers and I are going to set up a business marketing products manufactured by big names in the electronics field, and we would like an outlet here in Nigeria. I thought you might like to set up your own business and be our agent.'

'I'm thrilled at your suggestion, Mr Wang, but I've no experience whatsoever in the setting up of a business.'

'I'm aware of that. One has to start somewhere. The important thing was finding out if you would be interested in the project. I had a good look around both here in the office and elsewhere and you were the most reliable person I could approach. I've had the opportunity of working closely with you and I must say that I was impressed by your dedication to work and by your honesty.'

'I'm highly flattered, Mr Wang,' said Osifo, wondering why his last request for a wage increase was turned down if the General Manager had such a high opinion of him.

'Although,' continued Mr Wang, as if reading his thoughts, 'we're fully aware in this company that you're not as fully recompensed as you ought to be.

However, that's another matter. Now, about this project.'

'I imagine I'd need a huge amount of capital to set up a business like that.'

'Of course.'

'That's where the difficulty lies. I'm in no position to get a loan from a bank.'

'Why?'

'What I have in the bank is negligible and I've no property or Anything of the sort that would act as surety for a loan.'

'Don't worry about financial backing. I've thought about all that. Now, there's a Nigerian friend of mine who is willing to sponsor half the business and be a sleeping partner. He's a businessman from Gongola State and is reliable. For the other half. I'll help you secure a loan from a bank on fairly easy terms. This way, the business will belong to you and my friend. What is required of you is hard work and honest and efficient management. That's if you decide in favour of the project.'

'The proposal is very attractive, Mr Wang, and I'm very grateful for the opportunity you're giving me to set up on my own, but, if you don't mind. I'd like to think carefully about it before giving you my final word.'

'Fair enough. Think about it, discuss it with friends or relations and let me know your decision.* Shall we meet in two weeks' time? Will that do?'

'Oh yes. Thanks once again, Mr Wang.'

'I'm glad you're pleased, Mr Egie, but don't forget it works both ways and we are looking after our own interests too, that is, a good outlet for our products. So you're also doing us a favour.'

'It's kind of you to put it that way, Mr Wang.'

Osifo was happy at the prospect of setting up his own business yet he was scared of the responsibility. A lot of money would be involved. Could he handle it? What if he failed or went bankrupt? His father was more in favour of a steady salaried job. He felt Osifo was too young to set up a business of his own on such a large scale. It was too risky. Ifeanyi was all for it. 'Nothing ventured, nothing gained,' he reasoned.

After giving it a lot of thought, Osifo decided it would be foolish to miss such an opportunity. It would be good to be his own boss. All it required was dedication and a lot of hard work. He would need some luck too.

Having told Mr Wang of his decision, a meeting involving all the people concerned was held in Yola, after which Osifo left for Lagos to discuss the proposals with Wale, who was now a career diplomat and was married with three children.

Dipo Mwanga had disappeared suddenly three years before and no-one had ever heard of him since. Rumour had it that he had probably been murdered by enemies from his days as a party thug. This was never confirmed and he was never declared a missing person. Wale and Osifo missed him very much.

When the contract for the business was drawn up, Wale advised Osifo to contact a lawyer

who would go through it first before he finally
signed it.

Setting up a business, Osifo discovered, was a more
complicated process than met the eye. There were
so many things to do.

His partner, Mr Ahmed, the businessman
from Gongola State, suggested they call in a
management consultant who would advise them on
what was required. This they did and the company,
Medegie Electronics Company Limited, was set up
in Benin City.

One of the things he learnt during the
eighteen months it took for the company to be
established, was never to undermine the power of
the junior clerk in any organisation. The papers for
the registration of the company were half-way
through being processed when he was told, one
morning when he called at the Ministry, that his file
was missing. Two weeks later, it was still the same
story. The file could not be found. Furious, he went

to the Head of the Division, who was a friend of Wale's, to report the matter. The junior clerk responsible was called in, told off, and asked to look for it.

Another two weeks went by and the file had still not been found. The clerk was very sweet and polite about it all. He had searched everywhere but could not find it. Perhaps Mr Egie should start all over again, fill in fresh application forms and . . .

'Oh no,' cried Osifo at the suggestion. Start all over again! It had taken them three months to get that far. To get the application forms was a tug of war. The lady who gave them out was forever away from her desk, and no-one else could perform the feat in her absence. To get someone to hand them over to completion was another matter, and you had to chase your papers from one officer to the other and . . . When the clerk saw how dejected Osifo looked, he relented.

"Oga?'

'Yes?'

'Why did you report me to my boss?'

'Er . . . er . , since you could not find my file and things seemed to drag on, I thought he might be able to help.'

'But he could do nothing. Right? He couldn't come and search for it. If I said the file was missing, it was missing.' Osifo kept silent. He didn't know what to say to that. 'And if I say it has been found, then it has been found.' The clerk looked at him meaningfully. Osifo understood at last and some naira changed hands. The missing file surfaced promptly and everyone was satisfied.

Medegie Electronics was opened by a high official in the Bendel State Ministry of Commerce. Mr Wang came from Hong Kong for the occasion and Osifo's parents, brother and sisters and their families were at the high table. Mr Ahmed was there too. Wale was the master of ceremonies and his wife Yemisi, a caterer, organised the refreshments. Many important people attended.

Later that night while having drinks with Osifo at his flat nearby. Wale told him that what he needed more than anything else now was a wife by his side.

'Oh no,' cried Osifo. 'A wife! Not yet, old man. I don't want to be tied down.'

'Tied down to what?'

'To a woman and the responsibility that goes with being married. I'm not ready for all that yet.'

'Oh, come, Osifo, grow up. You're thirty or more now and cannot continue to play around forever. After a hard day you'd like to come home to a loving wife, and later the kids will come along and you'll feel very fulfilled.'

'Maybe you're right. Fll give it some serious thought.'

'Why? Aren't you and Betty going to get married? You seem quite fond of each other?'

'I'm fond of her all right, but I virouldn't like her for a wife. She's too shallow. She's good to be seen with at parties, but she can't give me the love and warmth I'd like from a wife. Besides, she's a lousy cook.'

'Hm! What about Esohe?'

'Oh, come again! She won't marry me even if I ask her. She adores money and I don't have any. She's told me several times that I'm the poorest man she's ever dated.'

'Why does she bother to be with you then?'

'I don't know. Perhaps there's something about me that she likes.'

'What about Kate? She looked lovely tonight.'

'She's a fool. Anything beyond clothes and parties is Greek to her. Look Wale, let's not run down the list of my girlfriends,' he laughed. 'My parents gave up trying to get me to get married ages ago. I won't hesitate when I meet the lady who can tolerate me. It won't be easy for whoever marries me, though.'

'Why? You look harmless to me.'

'Yes, but you see, I cannot really fall in love. Something always seems to hold me back. It dates back to a relationship I had with a lady when I was only a teenager. The way she treated me still rankles. I can't let myself go.'

'Oh, don't worry. I was like that until I met Yemisi. Even after several years of marriage we're still in love.'

'You're lucky.

'Yes, we both are. She's great and she makes me feel great in every way. Have I told you we've been posted to Zimbabwe? We shall leave next month.' 'No! Oh, I'll miss you so much.'

'We'll miss you too. You must come and see us.' 'I surely will. '

# Chapter 4

Ndidi and Seju were the last to leave the send-off party organised in their honour by a group of friends in London. As they drove through the chilly morning air to their flat in Tottenham in North London, Ndidi touched her husband's arm.

'Yes, darling?' he asked lazily.

'Nothing.' They looked at each other and laughed. He put his left arm around her, drew her close and tried to kiss her.

'Hey, look out! The lights are red! Stop!'

'Sorry, love,' he said as he quickly applied his brakes. 'The last thing we want is to be booked by the police on the eve of our departure from Britain. He drew her into his arms and kissed her passionately. The lights turned green and a car hooted behind them.

'Hm, nice,' he said, releasing her and driving off.

'Lovely. I must look like a wreck,' she giggled, peering at the mirror.

'You'll always look lovely to me,' he said affectionately, casting a sidelong glance at her. 'Any where, any time, even when you're old and grey,' he added.

'Same thing here,' said Ndidi, smiling, her heart full of love for him.

Her mind went back to the day they first met at a dance at the Africa Centre. It was summer and a popular Nigerian band on tour in Britain had been hired for the occasion by one of the numerous Nigerian societies based in London, who had organised the dance. The dance hall had been packed full with nostalgic African and Caribbean citizens who were anxious for a taste of 'home' music and atmosphere.

Many of them were students. Seju and Ndidi had both been dancing with their respective partners when their eyes met and that was it. It had been love at first sight for both of them. They did not speak but kept darting glances at each other, to the irritation of their partners. She had gone home that night deeply disappointed that he had made no move to get acquainted with her. But some days later he had turned up at the flat she shared with a friend and the relationship had taken off at a high tempo. Even after the wedding he still refused to tell her how he had got her name and address. When they met he was twenty-six and a part-time Engineering student at a technical college in South London. His father, who had sent him abroad for further studies, had died during his first year and Seju had had to take up a clerical job with the Post Office to support himself. He shared a flat with three other Nigerian students in Brixton. He took his studies seriously and worked hard and well.

Ndidi was twenty-two and was studying Accountancy at a school in Oxford Street. Her father, Chief Ugo Amengo, a prominent lawyer in Bendel State and a member of the National House of Assembly, was sponsoring her. She shared a flat with Denise, a Filipino girl who was studying Business Administration at the same school. When she realised how hard up financially Seju was, Ndidi offered to help him with money, but he had refused bluntly. He would not even let her pay her own half of the meals they had out, saying that it was carrying civilisation and women's lib too far when a man took a lady out and then allowed her to pay for herself. What was the point in taking her out in the first place? At first she thought his attitude was ridiculous. She would want to go to the pictures or the theatre or to a dance but couldn't because he could not afford it, and was too proud to let her pay for both of them.

Once, when he had noticed how disappointed she was, he had suggested that she go alone or with friends to the particular play she wanted to see. This had brought on their very first quarrel, as she had burst into tears saying he did not love her enough or he would not have suggested such an outrageous thing. Seeing the play with the man she loved was quite different from seeing it with friends or alone. She loved him and wanted them to spend all their free time together. He had been surprised at her outburst, but had gently insisted that he couldn't afford to pay and wasn't going to let her pay for the two of them. Later, she came to accept the situation.

He proposed to her on the first anniversary of their meeting, and she accepted. They both had one more year to go in their studies and they decided they would get married as soon as they graduated. Shouldn't your parents have met him first before you accepted him?' asked Denise when she was told the good news and shown the engagement ring. 'Oh, it doesn't matter,' said Ndidi happily. 'This is the twentieth century, you know. He'll meet my parents in due course. They'll like him and accept him once they know how much in love we are. After all, all they want is my happiness. I know I'll find it in Seju.'

That's true. He's a nice boy. If I were getting married to a boy from my country, he'd have to meet my people first before proposing to me. Marrying a foreigner is different, of course. You see, in my country, sometimes marriages are arranged between families.'In mine, too. But these days, that practice is diminishing and goes on mostly in the rural areas. Many young people in my country refuse to be forced into arranged marriages. Maybe that's why there are more happy marriages nowadays.'

Do you think so? I thought arranged marriages lasted longer.'Longer perhaps, but they're not necessarily happier. A relationship like marriage should be a fairly happy one even if it lasts for just one year. Afterwards you'd have the satisfaction that it had been nice. But to be together for a long time and be miserable with each other, it seems to me, is sheer folly.'

They had been going out for almost two years when Ndidi's parents came to London on holiday and were introduced to Seju. Later, when he asked Chief Amengo for permission to marry his daughter, Seju was refused. The Chief did not conceal his dislike for the young man. What have you against him, Popsie?' asked Ndidi, angry at the way her man had been dismissed.

'I don't like him.'

'But I love him very much.'

'You do, do you? Well, I don't blame you for that. I would fall in love with him myself if I were a woman. He's handsome, has nice manners and a bright future.'

'Well, there you are, Popsie,' said Ndidi, cooling down somewhat.

'He's a very likeable young man, I must say,' put in Mrs Amengo.

'But I wouldn't marry him,' continued the Chief as if the women had not spoken.

'Why ever not?' asked Ndidi, surprised.

For one, you know absolutely nothing about him, his background, his family.'Oh, that doesn't matter in the least. I'm not marrying his family, I'm marrying him. It's what he and I feel about each other that matters. Don't be childish, Ndidi. When you marry a man, in the African context, you are also marrying his family. You are marrying into a family of which you will become a member. Now, in fairness to yourself, before joining a club you have to find out more about it — if the ideals suit you and so on. You know very well what we in our family expect of our wives, but you don't know what pertains in Seju's family. Then, his background; there may be madness or leprosy in his family.'

It wouldn't matter to me. I love him and he loves me,' said Ndidi stubbornly.

'He probably wants to marry you because he knows that your father is rich and an important member of society. Well, not rich,' he amended hastily, not wanting his daughter to ask for a rise in her allowance later, 'eh, certainly not rich, but important. Yes, he would like to be the son-in-law of a member of the House of Assembly. I could sense it in his behaviour. I doubt it, Popsie. He knew almost nothing about my family when he proposed to me. Besides, you're not flattering me at all. Isn't there anything in me that makes him like me for myself? Something not connected with money and position? Something that made him fall in love with me the very first day he saw me? Well, listen to me, my daughter. To me you're a very pretty and intelligent woman. Any man can easily see that. We, your parents, are very proud of you in all respects. Now, marriage is a serious step in anyone's life, so you don't walk into it blindly. If you're sure both of you want to get married, wait until you get back to Nigeria and you've met his people. He's met us, and besides it's easier for the man. He doesn't have to fit into our family. I don't believe in these made-abroad marriages. Most of them disintegrate when faced with the realities at home. What do you have to say about all this, Martha?' he asked his wife.

You're right, Papa Ndidi,' she said. 'I like the young man. Although he's not from our tribe, I think he's nice. All the same, we know nothing of his family. I think his people should be thoroughly investigated. In fact, they should come to you and ask for our daughter's hand. It is to them that we give or refuse to give our daughter, not to him. Well, if that's the case,' said Ndidi, 'I'll tell Seju to write home to his people. They'll come and see you, Popsie. Please don't be difficult. I love him very much. I'm twenty-four now and I should know what I want.'

'All right, if that's what you want,' said her father sadly. 'Something still tells me that he's not the right man for you. He has a shifty look about him.'

'Popsie, there's nothing shifty about Seju,' laughed Ndidi, relieved that she had won the day. 'It's because you're a lawyer that you regard most people with suspicion. Why, most of my friends are green with envy. He's tops.'

'Hm!'

They got married in a Londop registry office. Ndidi's mother and her four brothers, who were studying in various parts of Europe at the time, attended the wedding, but her father did not. 'It's my small way of showing disapproval of the whole thing,' he wrote to her later. After their graduation and wedding, the couple stayed in Britain for about eighteen months, working and saving money to buy the things they would set up home with when they got back to Nigeria.

Ndidi discovered quite early that being a wife was quite a different kettle of fish from being a girlfriend. Being the former involved a lot of responsibility. You had to look after the man and the home. Although she had not strictly been born with a silver spoon in her mouth, she had been brought up where the bulk of the housework was done by maids, and as a student she had done very little housekeeping. So, the first few months were tough for her as she struggled with these duties.

Yet, on the whole, it was a blissful period for them because they were very fond of each other. Seju was a considerate man who took his duties as a husband seriously. They were so close to each other that they decided not to start a family right away, as they considered a third party would be an intruder at that stage.

When they got back to Nigeria, they settled in Lagos. He got a job with a construction company and she with a bank. They found a small flat in Yaba and life continued very much as before, for they had no serious problems. Ndidi had been a bit apprehensive about her husband's relations, but most of them, including his mother, were residing in Bendel State, and even when they visited, which was rare, they did not interfere.

The only problem she had, which she considered slight at the outset, was Seju's friends. They were of a different breed from the ones she had been used to abroad. There, most of the couples they knew did things together. On weekends and on public holidays, you took your family out and you all had a nice time. It did not matter if you had no money to go out to posh places. Even a stroll in the park armed with fish and chips was something, as what was important was the warmth of being together. Back home things were different, she noticed. Many men did not feel obliged to take out their families. They did their own thing and left the wives and kids to amuse themselves as best as they could. The wives, too, not wanting to be tied down to howling and bored children after a hard week, went out on their own. Most of Seju's friends were in the category of those who left their families at home. She never met the wives of many of them even though these men were forever popping in for visits and dragging Seju out with them.

It was when invitations to parties addressed only to Seju began to arrive that she sat up and began to take notice of things. She thought it was rude of the senders when they knew he was married. He thought nothing of it, explaining lightly that most of those parties were men-only affairs and women would be bored stiff there. Ndidi knew that it was taboo to take wives to parties like those for a bachelor's eve or toasting a new baby and so she did not worry too much when he sometimes went out alone, although it meant spending some Saturday nights by herself in the flat.

However, she was shocked one day when she asked as usual what they were going to do at the weekend and he told her casually that he was going to spend it in Lome. She was excited. She had never been to a francophone country before. Dear Seju! He had meant it as a surprise!

'Oh, that's lovely, darling,' she gushed. 'Do we need visas? Are we going by road?'

'We? I'm going by road with some of my friends.'

'Er, what do you mean, Seju?'

'I mean I'm spending this weekend in Lome with my friends.'

'What about me?' she asked, astonished that he had not bothered to tell her of his plans.

'You? You'll do what my friends' wives are doing, that is, stay behind,' he said carelessly.

'Why?'

'Why not? Must you follow me everywhere like Mary's lamb? Already my friends refer to you as my shadow. "Seju, are you coming to the party alone or will your shadow accompany you as usual?" It's embarrassing,'

What's embarrassing? We've always planned our outings together. It's normal. Why should what your friends think affect our relationship? Don't you know your own mind any more?' she said, flaring up. 'I don't actually mind you going off with your friends but you should have had the courtesy of letting me know of your plans. I'm supposed to be your wife, you know.'

'Look here,' he said, flaring up too, 'I think I've indulged you too much by consulting you about anything I want to do and in taking you out frequently. How many husbands do that? This is not Europe, you know. You can't dictate to me. You're always trying to wear the trousers in this house. I'm a master here and I'll do precisely what I like.'

'I see. Well, don't expect me to accept the situation.'

What will you do? Is it because your father is a lawyer that you are so pompous? My mother did warn me about that. You think of nothing else but of being taken out. It is because you're not gainfully employed. Now, if we had children like other couples, you'd be too busy to . . .'

'So, that's it! Now, whose idea was it that we should not start a family yet?'

'Mine, I agree, but that was two years ago.'

'Quite. You said we should spend the first five years on our own, because you wanted our children to come when we could comfortably afford them.

I agreed with you. We even decided we'd have just two when the time came. You did not tell me you had changed your mind since then.'

'That's true, but it's unnatural for a woman to accept having to wait that long. My mother said perhaps you can't have . . .'

'For crying out loud! Now, what's happening, Seju? Are you trying to ruin this marriage? If you want us to start a family why can't you discuss it with me? Why with your mother?'

The argument went on and on until Seju slammed the door and went out. He did have his weekend in Lome too, although he came back miserable and apologetic. Ndidi forgave him and for a while things were fine, but her confidence in their love had been shaken and she said they would start a family only when Seju was quite sure that that was what he wanted, for she did not believe that the arrival of babies would automatically improve a deteriorating marriage. The couple had to sort out their problems first. She felt it was important that child¬ ren should be brought into a loving atmosphere.

They began to drift apart gradually without realising it, except that they became aware that they no longer knew each other's plans. Seju was going out alone more and more, and making frequent weekend trips to Sapele. After a few arguments about it, Ndidi left things alone and began to develop other interests to keep herself busy. She took up tennis and swimming and took lessons in flower arrangement.  When she complained about Seju's behaviour to her mother during one of the latter's trips to Lagos, she was told not to be so fussy over trivial matters. Seju is a good man,' said her mother. 'He's a responsible husband. He pays the rent, he gives you money for housekeeping and he buys you presents. You told me so yourself.'

Yes, Mama, but that's not all there is to a marriage, I hardly know him any more. He's changed drastically. We used to be so close. Now, he hardly discusses his plans with me and he's always out. I'm only like a housekeeper here now.'

'Is another woman involved? Doesn't he take all his meals at home?'

'He takes most of his meals here. I don't know if there's another woman for I've never bothered to find out, and I don't encourage gossip about such matters. '

'Well, if he does have another wife, it doesn't matter so long as he continues to take good care of you. By the way, are you still going to wait for ten years before having a baby? Not ten years, Mama. The atmosphere in the home has to improve before bringing children into it.

Atmosphere? What atmosphere? Aren't you happy? You're lucky to have such a good husband. Why, Rose Okafor, your childhood friend, was thoroughly beaten and sent out of the house by her husband last month, but she's back now. Her people went to beg him to take her back and, after a severe warning, he did.'

It was no use. Her mother wouldn't understand. Paying the rent and supplying money for housekeeping was more important to her than love and companionship. She didn't blame her mother though, for that was the point of view held by most women of her generation. Financial security was all that mattered. Ndidi wanted more than that from a marriage, for after all, she could afford to look after herself comfortably if the need arose. What she wanted was to be one with the man she loved. Otherwise, what was marriage all about? Although she believed in women's lib, she also believed that the man should be the boss in the home, but in partnership with the woman. She admired men who knew their own mind and took firm decisions. Her Seju was easily swayed by what friends and relations thought. It actually upset him not to toe other people's lines and he tried to make up for this defect by being extremely forceful about things at home.

Ndidi began to despise him. She could see a future in which the major decisions in the family were influenced by other people. There would be constant friction, for they both had a stubborn streak in their character. Seju had not stopped loving his wife. He had no doubt in his mind about that. How he wished things could continue the way they had been abroad. Both of them had been very close and what they did was their own business. Here things were different. If you were constantly seen in the company of your wife, then you were 'tied to her wrapper'; you were 'not a man in your own home'. He hated criticism and particularly criticism from his mother, who pretended to accept Ndidi but who actually disliked her intensely because her son loved the girl and was happy with her. She had had an unhappy polygamous marriage in which she had been the neglected wife, even though she was the one who produced the heir. This had made her very bitter. Seju was ail she had and she was jealous of Ndidi's self-confidence and happiness.

Moreover, she was afraid that her son might be 'swallowed up' by her daughter-in-law's more prominent family, so she did her best to destroy the union. She wanted a daughter-in-law she could have under her thumb. She found such in Gbemi, a neighbour's daughter whom Seju had known all his life. This girl was twenty-three, pretty in a dark slim way, and was a teacher in one of the local schools in Sapele. She was shy and unassuming. Whenever Seju came down from Lagos, he would find Gbemi in the house helping his mother with the chores.

Later on she began to prepare his meals and wash his clothes. At first, he took her out as a neighbourly gesture, then gradually a relationship developed. He was not in love with her, but she was a contrast to his lively wife, so her shyness and modesty sometimes came as a relief to him. On the rare occasions that Ndidi had accompanied him to Sapele, Gbemi did not call, so she never knew of the other's existence. When a friend told her that a girl in Sapele was expecting a baby by her husband, it did not come as a surprise to Ndidi. It explained all those trips there. She was shattered, of course, but she found that it was not as awful as she had always imagined such a situation would be. Could it be the result of the gap that existed in their relationship?

When asked, Seju readily admitted the affair, and even with obvious relief, for he had been at a loss as to how to broach the topic to her. She looked at her husband. He was like a stranger. She could not even remember having seen the shirt he had on before, and she used to buy all his shirts and ties. Where had their love gone? When had they stopped loving each other? What has gone wrong? Whose fault was it? Would things have been different if they had remained abroad, far away from interfering with friends and relations? These questions were going through her mind when she suddenly realised that Seju had left the room. Later, she heard him drive off. There had been no remorse, no apology, no explanation! She sat down in the dark room and cried a bit over their lost love. What was she to do? Should she stay put and hope that the affair would die out? But how? A child was involved, so the relationship could never really be wiped out. Anyway, could she really remain in such a loveless atmosphere?

Seju solved the problem a month later when he sought and obtained a transfer to Minna. He did not invite Ndidi along with him. He simply packed his things and left. His mother promptly went to live with him, taking Gbemi with her.

Ndidi stayed on in Lagos for some months afterwards while she reorganised herself. Then she resigned from her job and moved to Benin City. Her parents were sympathetic, but there was little they could do for her. She became restless, and in the course of one year she changed jobs twice. She kept blaming herself for the failure of her marriage. She ought to have made more effort to save it. She should have come off the pill and started a family. Had she actually been too proud? Perhaps she . . .

What hurt her most was that Seju had made no move to communicate with her in any way since he moved out. How could he have cut her out of his life like that? It was callous! It was as if they had never met. The next three months were traumatic. She became very ill and had to go into hospital. When she got better her mother took her to Ute to recuperate, and after about a month there she was well enough to return to Benin City. She moved into a flat of her own and began to look for a job. But it took her nearly four months to find something suitable. She had come to terms with herself and had stopped frequent thoughts about Seju and their broken marriage. No-one brought her news of him and she did not inquire about him.

Many months afterwards she got a letter from a solicitor informing her that Seju had filed a suit for a divorce. She handed it to one of the lawyers in her father's chambers for a follow-up and tried to settle down to a new life.

She loved her new job which involved a lot of responsibility and was more challenging than anything she had had so far. She threw herself into it and shut out most other things. The only time she relaxed was during her monthly trips to the company's other branches outside Benin City. After a business trip, she always took one day off. This she spent as she liked, either sightseeing or just lazing around. She was thankful she had no children yet, for it would have meant frequently leaving them in the care of someone else, and this she would have hated to do. As it was, she had only herself to look after and so it did not matter if she spent most of her time on the job. It was during one of these trips that she had met Gogo. They had had adjoining seats on the plane from Lagos to Port Harcourt. He was a tall thin man, but handsome in a delicate way. A woman's first instinct on seeing him was to take him away somewhere, feed him and look after him forever.

Ndidi did not usually like being chatted up in a plane by men because she believed they used the intimate atmosphere to pick up ladies, and this made her feel cheap. But on this occasion, seeing Gogo sitting there gazing sadly into space, her curiosity was aroused. He looked so vulnerable. Could he be dumb and deaf? She did not know that this was one of the ploys he used to attract the ladies, for he was a playboy. If the soulful look did not work then he would switch on his 'chatty' seif. A lady had to be very strong not to fall for one or the other. At first she ignored him, but when he refused his tea, his breakfast and a drink, she had to ask him if he was sick. He shook his head sadly. She ignored him again. His silence irritated her. 'What is the matter then?' she asked, in spite of herself. He quickly came alive and brought out a pocket pad. 'I would like to know you, but I'm a very shy man', he wrote. They both burst out laughing.

Within ten minutes he had extracted from Ndidi her name and address, and where she was staying in Port Harcourt. He told her he was an architect based in Warri and that he was roaming about looking for contracts. He was so funny that Ndidi thawed. He was the first man to interest her since Seju. That evening he turned up at her hotel dressed in the traditional attire of the Delta area — a wrapper, a loose silk shirt, coral beads, a hat with a feather tucked in it, sandals and a walking stick. He looked elegant and a bit older than his thirty-five years. He led her to a sleek sports car, and then they were off to explore the town. There wasn't really much to see, but he was so full of enthusiasm as he took her from place to place that she didn't want to spoil it all by telling him that she would rather sit down for a drink and a chat. As she crawled into her bed in the early hours of the morning, she wondered if she hadn't bitten off more than she could chew by taking on someone like Gogo. He was so restless, yet he was such a charmer that it had been nice to be swept along in his zest for life.

When they returned to Bendel State, he began courting her in earnest. He often came down to Benin City on business or to spend the weekend. She found that despite his funny ways he was dedicated to his work. He told her that he had seven children from two broken marriages, lots of girl friends but that she was special to him. She did not know whether to take him seriously or not but she grew quite fond of him and the relationship continued. Although she had always been a 'one man' girl, this time she occasionally dated other men, because she was scared of getting deeply involved with Gogo who was becoming more and more possessive. He would sulk no end whenever he was in town and she was out with another guy. This amused her. She couldn't understand why such a thing bothered him, for after all they weren't married and he had his other girls.

He began to get serious. He wanted them to go steady and get engaged. She was fond of him but marriage was very far from her mind; certainly not when the scars from the final days of her time with Seju were still very fresh. In fact she had half made up her mind to forget about marriage and to have relaxed and enjoyable relationships only. Anyway, could she cope with a man with seven children who was a notorious playboy to boot?

# Chapter 5

Medegie Electronics Company Limited was now five years old and was beginning to make a profit after three difficult years of barely meeting its overheads. The company had moved to new premises on the Benin Sapele Road where they hoped to have an assembly plant in the future if business continued to be good. Osifo, as the Managing Director, had worked really hard to get things going, and his partner and Chairman, Mr Ahmed, was pleased. So also was Mr Wang, their major supplier. The company had branches in Yola, Kaduna and Port Harcourt. Osifo was leading a fairly comfortable life now. He lived in a large company house in a good area, with a tennis court and a swimming pool. He had a driver, a cook and a gardener. In short he had everything befitting the chief executive of a moderately successful company. His family were fiercely proud of him.

Life for his parents had at last become comfortable. There was no more tiresome farmwork for them; Osifo and Ifeanyi had converted the old house into a semi-modem one and Chief Amengo had fulfilled his election campaign promises to his constituency of pipe-borne water and electricity.

Their greatest joy came when Osifo took them on a three-week holiday to Europe and the USA. This had cost him a whole year's savings, and even then, his brothers and sisters had had to contribute their share. But it had been well worth it, for it gave him great pleasure to watch the delight on his aged parents' faces as they marvelled at almost everything they saw. For years afterwards, they kept their friends in the village spellbound with stories of the 'magic in the Whiteman's cities'. They were never tired of showing slides of their tour. The only dark cloud in their sky was Osifo's seemingly permanent state of bachelorhood. They could not understand why at thirty-four he still said that he had not met the right woman. Who was this right woman he was waiting for? At the rate he was going, they told him they were unlikely to have grandchildren from him before they died. He laughed off their fears, saying that they had many more years to live, and that anyway they already had lots of grandchildren to surround themselves with.

He was not short of girls, but while not actually changing them like ties, as he had promised himself years before when he had little time for them, he did have his fun and was happy, even though it was becoming increasingly embarrassing that there was no hostess at the parties they gave. Mr Ahmed told him it gave the company a bad image if the Managing Director had no wife. People would think he was queer or something. What made the matter worse was that he had no children either. Once he overheard some girls discussing him at a party. 'Oh, something is definitely wrong with Mr Egie,' said one. 'At his age he's never been married. It's strange.'

'Yes, it is. It will be tough for whoever marries him.'

'Why?'

'He must be set in his bachelor habits now and he will find it difficult to adjust to married life.'

'That's true, especially if he's not virile.'

'Yes, what a pity!'

Osifo smiled slowly. Not virile indeed! But he was not going to let what people think push him into getting married, he said to himself stubbornly. He wanted a twin soul like that which Wale had found in Yemisi. He did have a fairly steady relationship with Itohan, a veterinary surgeon with the Ministry of Agriculture. She was a pretty, sophisticated girl of about twenty-five and he was quite fond of her, which was the closest he had been to being in love with any woman. Several times, he had been on the point of proposing to her, but he always held back. He felt there wasn't sufficient affection between them to sustain a marriage, and yet he couldn't stop seeing her. Sometimes he wondered if he wouldn't do well to marry her and start a family. At the back of his mind his rejection by Madam Adunni still rankled, although only faintly now. Did he really have to be in love with the woman he married? What would happen when there was no more love between them? Was it not better to avoid the heart being involved? That way there would be no heartache.

He wasn't sure. As part of the expansion and development of the company, Osifo had gone on a nine-month management course to Europe and the Far East. Now, he was back and was itching to get on with the job. He went to work very fresh and eager to absorb everything. Things had run fairly smoothly in his absence and Mr Shyllon, the Area Manager for Kaduna who had deputised for him, had performed his duties satisfactorily. All the same, Osifo regarded the company as his 'baby' and so was anxious to take over the reins once more. 'It wouldn't do to let people think I'm dispensable here,' he told himself.

The first week was pretty hectic as he struggled to get a grasp of everything that had been omitted from the regular monthly report he had received during his stay abroad. It was amazing how many important things were termed as 'trivial' and left out of reports. For example it was mentioned briefly that a new Accountant/Administration Manager had been appointed to take the place of the previous one who had embezzled company money and had been asked to resign his appointment. But no names were given. He was really astonished when the Personnel Manager, Mr Idahosa, introduced a woman to him as the new Accountant/ Administration Manager. His managers knew very well his sentiments about having to work closely with female staff. He just couldn't cope with it. In fact after a succession of female secretaries he had opted for a male one, and things had run smoothly ever since. No more 'off days' every month and unexplained absences or long personal conversations on the telephone. The work was done. He wanted absolutely no-one, and certainly not a female, messing up a company he had carefully built up. He didn't mind women in top positions so long as he didn't have to work too closely with them. Let their attitude to work be someone else's headache. In his company, he had always worked very closely with the Accountant, and he had had a very good working relationship with Mr Otabor, the previous one. Although the man was a cheat, he had worked conscientiously otherwise and that was why for many months Osifo had overlooked his malpractices and only given him verbal warnings.

When Osifo was introduced to the lady, he hid his surprise well, spoke pleasantly to her and welcomed her into the company, but as soon as she left the room he gave full vent to his annoyance.

'Now, what did you do such a thing for?' he asked Mr Shyllon and Mr Idahosa. 'You never mentioned it in the report.'

'What, Mr Egie?' asked Mr Shyllon.

'Employ a lady as an accountant here! You know full well I cannot work closely with women, and also that I have to work quite closely with anyone in that particular position. I regularly need to see the accountant at short notice, whether in the office or at home, and often we have to work late together. How do you expect me to have such a working relationship with a lady? Ridiculous!'

'I'm sorry, Mr Egie,' said Mr Shyllon. 'I accept full responsibility for the appointment. You see, she is highly qualified for the job and she was the best of the lot we interviewed. She had excellent references from the branch of the bank with which she worked in Lagos. Besides, I've had no problem with her in the six months she's been here.'

'She works hard and things have improved in the Accounts and the Administration departments,' put in Mr Idahosa. 'I don't care. Sack her! I don't want a female accountant. It would be too much trouble. Imagine this: I'll have to knock on the door each time I want to go into her office; I'll have to watch my language when things aren't going too well so as not to reduce her to tears; I'll have to put up with numerous excuses for late-coming and absences. Of course she cannot work late or on weekends because of her husband and the children. How do we get any work done? Ridiculous!'

'She's not married,' said Mr Idahosa, 'or rather, she's divorced with no children. She works late sometimes, but I don't think she needs to as her work is always up to date.'

'She's divorced, you said? That's even worse — the frustrated female. She'll spend hours on end on the telephone, calling up one boyfriend after the other, or plainly gossiping with others like herself. I might tolerate that from a typist or a clerk, but certainly not from an accountant. Has she been confirmed yet?'

'No. She has three more months to go.'

'No problem then. Simply don't confirm her appointment. Get rid of her on some pretext or other.'

'That would be difficult now that she has been written a letter saying we're satisfied with her work and that the second part of her probation has begun.'

'Who wrote that?'

'I did,' said Mr Idahosa. 'It's routine.'

'Let's hope she'll embezzle some company money as her predecessor did and she'll get the

sack.' 'I doubt if Miss Amengo will do that, 'said Mr Shylion. 'What would she need the money for?

She has only herself to look after. Besides, I think she's honest.'

'So was her predecessor until two years ago when he started building a new house. He had been a conscientious worker until then and I rather liked him. Do tell me. Is this Miss Amengo any relation to Chief Amengo the lawyer?'

'I don't know,' said Mr Shyllon, 'but I understand her father is a member of the National Assembly.'

'Then she's Chief Amengo's daughter. Wait a minute! Is her first name Ndidi?'

'Yes. Do you know the family?'

'Yes, I know Chief Amengo although I've not seen him for some time, and I've met Ndidi once. So, that was Miss Hoity-toity! Hm! When I last saw her she was all legs and pimples. Quite haughty and insolent she was too.'

'Well, don't let that count against her now. She's a fine lady.'

'I see that you like her.'

'I do. I think she's an asset to the company. She works very hard and is quite reliable. You'll enjoy working with her, since you like to work hard too.'

'I doubt if I'll enjoy working with her, but I'll give her a chance, since she has such glowing recommendations from you both.'

Osifo tried as hard as he could to find flaws in Ndidi's work, but he could not. She carried out her duties efficiently and worked late when asked to. Her only fault was that she was perhaps too strict with the workers, but then he could not really complain about that. She had lowered the formerly high rate of absenteeism since she took over and loafing about during office hours had almost stopped. Sometimes he wondered if she was really as hard as she made out. Perhaps the staff did need an iron hand in order to be made to sit up. However, he still did not think a woman was right for the position, and the fact that she was Chief Amengo's daughter did not help matters. He had not forgotten the way the Chief treated his workers. His mother's cousin who worked at the factory in Ute said that conditions were still bad there. Although the factory had expanded and was making a profit, the workers were still among the lowest paid in the country, and whenever they asked for better conditions of service, the Chief would threaten to shut down the factory. The people could hardly afford this since there was high unemployment in the area. To them half a loaf was better than no loaf at all.

Osifo also resented the way the Chief had cast aside his father who had helped him immensely during his first election campaign. Not only did the Chief fail to show appreciation for his friend's help, but having established a foothold in that constituency, he ignored Mr Egie and began to deal directly with the village heads and elders who had been introduced to him by his friend in the first place. He hardly saw his old friend any more. Mr

Egie, on the other hand, was not offended by his friend's attitude. He was used to it. What pleased him was that he had given help satisfactorily when asked, and as far as he was concerned that was all that mattered.

Although he did not find her beautiful, certainly not in the fabulous way Itohan was, Osifo was not indifferent to Ndidi's charms. She was attractive, had a good figure and carried herself well; and those long, long legs. She had charming manners to go with them too. She appealed to him more now than she did as a teenager. Sometimes, when they sat working together and their knees or hands met accidentally, a shiver would run through him. This annoyed him as she never seemed to notice anything amiss. She never moved away nor took the slightest interest. He consoled himself by saying that he wouldn't be a man if sitting close to a pretty lady failed to stir up anything in him. But it was bad for work. He made it a point never to date any female in his establishment as this might lead to the lady concerned becoming heady and unco-operative towards her immediate bosses. It wasn't worth it.

However, perhaps this would be the best way to rid the company of Ndidi, he sometimes said to himself. He would date her a few times and then drop her. She was the proud type who would certainly not like to remain in the firm after such a thing had happened to her. But did he really have to go to such lengths? The whole thing would be too untidy, yet, something had to be done to put things right. Perhaps if he overworked her and she could not keep up with the pace, she would go of her own volition.

Ndidi thought Osifo pompous and overbearing. Why was he constantly anxious to show everyone that he was the boss in the place? She had heard that he built up the firm from scratch, but surely he could afford to relax a bit now. There was certainly no threat to his position from any quarter. Was it all a sign of insecurity? She found him intelligent, conscientious and full of confidence. All some bosses wanted to know from the accountant was how well or badly the company was doing financially, but Osifo wanted more than that and no detail was too minor for him. He took all the intricacies of accountancy in his stride.

She had no doubt that he could carry out the duties of an accountant well if the need arose. Later, she discovered that that was how he kept tabs on all the departments. He knew every employee by sight and name, and what his or her duties were. She enjoyed working with him, but was uneasy about his veiled resentment of her. She had been told that he did not want her in the company because she was Chief Amengo's daughter. But her father had never mentioned him to her even though he knew where she worked. Perhaps he did not know who the Managing Director was. Osifo had told her that he once spent the night with her family and that they had gone out together to a disco session, but she could not recollect having seen him before. During her father's early days in politics, they had entertained a lot and had many guests to stay, and it was impossible to recall every face.

One thing she was quite sure of was that Osifo was deliberately overworking her in order to edge her out of the company. She could cope with the work all right, but what she could not stand was unreasonableness. For instance, she got to the office one morning to find an airline ticket and a note from him telling her to take the 10.30 am flight to Kaduna for urgent business. But both of them had worked together late the previous evening and he had not breathed a word about the journey. When she checked, she found that the ticket had been purchased and the flight booked several days before. As Head of the Administration Department she was supposed to be in charge of travel. Her first reaction that morning was to say to hell with it all and stay put. She might have no family but that did not mean that she had no right to a planned life. Even a man could not be ordered about like that at a moment's notice. It wasn't as if what was involved was an emergency which couldn't last until the next working day which was a Monday. The trip would ruin the weekend which she and Gogo had planned to spend in Lagos. He was going to arrive late that afternoon and they were going to take the last flight out to Lagos. Now, all that would have to be altered. Gogo would be so mad. He hated his plans being messed up by others. She did, too.

She went to Kaduna anyway, after telling Gogo in a hurried note to proceed to Lagos and that she would take the first flight there from Kaduna the next day. At times, she thought she was altogether too eager to please Osifo. It was not as if she could not get another, and probably better paid. Job elsewhere if she were to leave Medegie Electronics. But why give the man the pleasure of seeing his plan work? If he wanted her out, then let him sack her. She would sue him for wrongful and malicious dis¬ missal and soak him for tens of thousands of naira. She would fight him with every kobo she had. Why must she always be the one to give in? She had given in meekly to Seju when news of Gbemi came.

Instead of asserting herself and causing lots of trouble for all concerned, she had merely accepted the situation and Seju had got off lightly — very lightly indeed — and she had been humiliated. She had thought then that she was reacting in a civilised manner. Not that she had had much choice in the matter, but at least, she would have had the satisfaction that other people had had a headache too. Anyway, the present situation was a much easier one since neither love nor affection was involved. She was going to stay on and only leave the company when it suited her to do so. She knew exactly when that would be, for she had decided to get even with Osifo for all this pushing around. She would hit him when it would hurt him most.

Meanwhile her relationship with Gogo had moved a step forward; she had stopped seeing other men and she and Gogo were now going steady, although she suspected that this was one-sided for she had a feeling that he still had other women in Warri and Port Harcourt. This did not bother her, for after all the stalling was on her side. He proposed to her steadily every other month and it became a standing joke as she turned him down on each occasion. Although he appeared serious about his intention to marry her, she did not think he could go through with it if accepted. He probably proposed to her to salve his conscience and assure both of them that he was not wasting her time. She felt he was too independent and too set in his ways to want to give up his freedom a third time. He would some day perhaps, when he was older and needed someone to take care of him, but not just yet.

Sometimes, she thought she should take the bull by the horns, accept him and settle down. At thirty, she felt she was not getting any younger. She knew that their marriage could be successful if she took things coolly and in a mature way. He was a very likeable person with his ready humour and relaxed view of life and besides he was successful. Her parents, particularly her father, liked him and were always asking her to bring him over for a meal or drinks whenever they were both in Lagos.

She smiled at the thought of her father. The old man had mellowed a lot since the arrival of a baby girl by his second wife, Eki, a twenty-two year old girl he had married two years before. Whenever he came down to Benin City, he liked nothing better in his spare time than to dandle the baby on his knees and coo endlessly to her. If he was thrilled about her, Ndidi's mother was besotted. As soon as Eki became pregnant she had gone to Europe on a shopping spree for both the mother-to-be and her child, and she took over control completely when the baby arrived, only allowing the mother to breast-feed her. Her devotion to both Eki and her child went deeper than just playing her role as 'senior wife', for she had actually chosen the bride for her husband from her own village, and she had paid the bride price. Eki called her 'Mama' and took any problem she had to her. Ndidi was 'sister' and the boys 'brother'. Eki liked the family into which she had married and counted herself luckier than most of her friends.

Not only was the family a wealthy one, the senior wife was kind. She had always known that she would marry Chief Amengo for as long as she could remember, £dl her expenses had been paid for by Mrs Amengo. She had left college in her second year when she kept failing her examinations and had told her parents she did not want to study any more, but Mrs Amengo had insisted she went to a catering school in Asaba. This she had done and had got married as soon as she had completed her studies. She lived in the Amengo family house in Benin City with Ndidi's paternal grandmother and a host of cousins. Sometimes, she would go and spend a week or two with Ndidi's parents who now lived most of the time in Lagos.

Eki tried her best to please the family. She went to Ndidi's flat every weekend to clean and cook. Ndidi, who liked her privacy, protested, but to no avail. The girl simply enjoyed doing things for Ndidi and her brothers. It was part of the culture in which she had been brought up, and to behave otherwise would have been strange. She in turn was well looked after by the family. She only had to express a wish and it was granted by one member or the other.

All these things reminded Ndidi of what her father had told her in London about a woman being 'married to the whole family' in the African context. It was true, although she doubted if she would be able to comply. It would be too much trouble, for not all families were nice or appreciative of such a service. Even though she was not yet married to Gogo, some of his relations had sometimes asked her to help out at family parties in Warri, and she had, but had hated every minute of it. She did not mind the work, but usually at these all-female gatherings, 'wives' were always given all the heavy duties while the 'daughters of the family' sat around all day giving orders, chatting, eating and doing very little work.

It made her feel like an unpaid servant. If a member of the family disliked you, you'd have it, for the occasion provided an opportunity for her to say jokingly aloud what she thought of you. You would be too embarrassed to answer back.

Osifo and Itohan were having a drink in his club one afternoon when Ndidi and Gogo came in. They were in tennis gear and were in the company of Remi Hardman, a fellow member. Although he had seen them together before, Osifo felt slightly annoyed on seeing Ndidi and Gogo arm in arm.

'I don't know what the fuss is all about. The man is a dandy and ought to be displayed in a glass case,' he said under his breath, eyeing Gogo's embroidered sports shirt with distaste.

'Hm?' asked Itohan, looking up from stirring her drink. 'Did you speak?'

'Eh, just thinking aloud.'

She saw Ndidi. 'Ah, here comes your accountant and her glamorous boyfriend or fiance. Which is he? Are they engaged?'

'I don't know,' he said, getting angry. 'I know nothing about her private life.'

Ndidi saw them and waved, then she whispered to Gogo and they walked over. She introduced both men and went over to Itohan for a little chat. Gogo towered above Osifo and spoke to him in a condescending manner. It reminded Osifo of 'Uncle Abiodun' of Madam Adunni days. However, he had built up a lot of confidence in himself since then, and such an attitude no longer worried him, so he merely smiled when Gogo said he was pleased to meet Ndidi's 'big white chief' at last. They looked at each other with barely concealed dislike.

'That's a nice shirt you have on,' remarked Osifo.

'Oh, thanks. You can't buy anything like it here. I had it made specially for me by a tailor in Hamburg.'

'Oh, I wouldn't want to buy it. It looks rather feminine. Some jester might even say you've got your wife's blouse on, but I must say it looks wonderful on you.'

'I've got the figure to carry it off,' said Gogo with pride.

'Precisely what I thought. On some men it would look cissy, but then . . .' said Osifo sweetly. He sat down and picked up his drink.

'What do you mean?' asked the other.

'In what way?'

Just then the girls finished their chat and the couple moved off, with Gogo throwing a look of daggers at the unperturbed Osifo.

'What was that for?' asked Itohan. 'He looked as if he could cheerfully murder you. What did you say to him?'

'I told him his shirt was nice. It seemed to make him angry.'

'That's strange. Perhaps you should have offered them a drink.'

'Why? They are not my guests. They are Remi's. Come on, let's drink up and go,'

Ndidi was confirmed in her position and things continued in very much the same way. Osifo still hadn't quite shelved his plan to replace her with a male accountant, only now there was no urgency. He had decided that when he got the right man, he would make him Financial Controller and Ndidi would have to report to him. If she did not like the new set-up, then she was free to withdraw her services. It would be a pity if she decided to go, for he now agreed with Mr Shyllon and Mr Idahosa that she was an asset to the company. She was one of the few managers that he could trust with money and confidential matters and in certain things he trusted only her and relied on her sense of judgment. He was amused when he was told by a colleague that some members of staff referred to her as 'Mr Egie's backbone'. Backbone indeed! Did he really rely on her that much? He knew that if he wanted things done the way he would have done them himself, then he could entrust them to her only. She had never disappointed him. She was co-operative and was eager to please him.

The way things were between herself and Osifo pleased Ndidi. She was pandering to most of his demands and he seemed to like it. She never grumbled when he gave her responsibilities outside her normal duties, or suggested outrageous working hours. What satisfied her most was the confidence and trust he had in her. 'He doesn't realise it yet,' she confided in Nimi, her bosom friend, 'but he's beginning to rely on me more and more to carry out important assignments for him.'

'What's wrong with that? You told me you enjoy working for him.'

'That's right, I do, but it's unwise of him to have so much trust in me.'

'Why?'

'I might betray him or let him down.'

'Well, would you?'

'I don't know. You see, it would be nice to hurt him for all these knocks I've been getting from him. He should realise I'm not a slave. He's selfish. He's after the interests of his wretched company all the time. He never bothers to find out whether it is convenient or not for me to work late or travel at a moment's notice. He just gives the orders,'

'But surely, Ndidi, you wouldn't go as far as betraying the trust he has in you in order to make him know that you don't like the way he treats you?'

'I might. That's why I've worked hard all these months to make him trust me.'

'That sounds hard and calculating and unlike you.'

'Well, that was the plan I had in mind when I realised that he didn't want me in the company. Now, I'm not so sure.'

'Tell me, why do you let him treat you as he does? You're normally a no-nonsense person. I overheard Gogo telling Martin the other day that he was getting fed up with the whole thing. He said that before you both plan an outing you've got to make sure first that Mr Egie did not require your services for that period. Is it true? Have things got as bad as that?'

'No, they haven't,' laughed Ndidi. 'Gogo was only exaggerating as usual. He dislikes Osifo.'

'Who's Osifo?'

'Mr Egie.'

'Oh, you're on first name terms, are you?'

'No. Only in my thoughts. Come on, Nimi, out with it! What are you suggesting?'

'Nothing. You watch out, my girl,' she said wagging a finger, 'you've probably fallen in love with him without realising it.'

Ndidi couldn't help bursting into laughter. 'Now, you've really said it, Nimi, Fall in love with him indeed! You're kidding! The man is unbearable and insensitive. Who would fall in love with a brick wall?'

'He has girlfriends.'

'Sure he does, but do they love him? Look at that piece of nuisance he goes about with. Itohan, or whatever her name is — the doctor of dumb animals. She's only after his money and position, if you ask me.'

'I don't think so. She has a good job and comes from a fairly rich family. She doesn't need his money. She must love him.'

'How can she love him? To love a man like Osifo you need a lot of patience and understanding to break through the defence he's built up all around him and Itohan looks pretty shallow to me, not the type to bother to study a man. She can't love him deeply, that's if she does love him at all. She's wasting her time too. He doesn't love her.'

'Hmmm, how do you know that? Does he discuss her with you?'

'No. I knew by intuition.'

'You must be in love with him then. I've never heard you speak so strongly against another woman. Do you dislike Itohan?'

'Not really, but I don't like the way she hangs around him. She should stick to her dumb friends.'

'Why? Well, never mind. But look out as I said. I can see the love-light in your eyes.'

'Ho! Ho! It's for Gogo and no-one else,'

# Chapter 6

Osifo hadn't realised how much Ndidi featured in his thoughts until the day he went shopping for some furniture and material for curtains to redecorate his house for the visit of Wale and his family. He couldn't make up his mind what to buy, wondering whether Ndidi would approve of this or that. At last, he raced back to the office to get her only to be told that she had left early for home because she had felt ill. His initial reaction was to rush to her flat, but on the way there, however, he decided not to. What would he say to her? 'What am I doing? I should be consulting Itohan about the choice of furniture, and not Ndidi.' So, he merely drove past her house and went home. When he asked her the next day if she was feeling better, she told him that she was all right and that it was Eki, her father's wife, who had been taken seriously ill and she had been sent for.

'Oh, I see. Wasn't there any other person with her at home?'

'What do you mean, Mr Egie?' she asked, flaring up. She had had a sleepless night by Eki's hospital bed and was quite tired. The man was inhuman!

'Er, since they had to send for you at work . . .'

'Ah, you mean that when my father's wife's life is in danger, and my parents are away, I should not be sent for? I should not leave my precious duties at Medegie Electronics to help a person who is seriously ill? Fm sorry Your Excellency for desert¬ ing my post for such a trivial matter.'

Take it easy, Ndidi,' he said, holding her arm as she made for the door of his office. 'Don't be offended. You did not allow me to finish my sentence.'

'You didn't need to,' she said, trying to shake herself free. But he held on firmly. 'You're quite insensitive and you're a slave-driver. I just can't believe that a human being could be so indifferent to other people's welfare. You seem to think that my entire life depends on this job. It doesn't, you know. I'm not starving. Far from it. I have my reasons for my continued stay here. You've never wanted me in this company. The way you overwork me is incredible, and I think I've had enough and so. I'll teU you what you can do with your job. She collapsed into a chair, exhausted from her outburst.

Osifo got her a cup of water and sat on the arm of her chair.

'Look, Ndidi, I'm sorry. As I was saying, you did not allow me to finish my sentence.'

'What were you going to say, Mr Egie?'

'Er, I've forgotten now. What I probably meant was that I hoped there was someone with her when she collapsed or something to that effect. I can assure you that your duties in the office did not come into my mind at all. I'm not callous, you know. You've got the wrong end of the stick.'

'Well, actually, Mr Egie, I know that you're quite kind and reasonable with people generally.

I've actually overheard some workers complain that I'm more difficult to please than the Managing Director. However, why do you drive me so hard with so much work?'

'Because I've a lot of trust in you.'

'But you have that same trust in one or two other managers.'

'Well, maybe it's because you let me drive you hard. You've never kicked.'

'Did you expect me to?'

'Sometimes, just to show that you're not a saint.'

'Fine. As from now, Mr Egie, I won't be that co-operative. I want my weekends free. My private life is suffering. As it is, I seem to live and breathe Medegie. My boyfriend is complaining, and he's right.'

'I'm sorry again. I was being selfish and a bit thoughtless in expecting you to work with me at weekends. We shall reschedule our work to exclude Saturdays.'

'Fine. Er ; . . er . . . but if you really do need me sometimes, I shall be glad to oblige,' she said, relenting somewhat while at the same time realising that she would miss those quiet working sessions they had at weekends.

'No, Ndi. A promise is a promise. Your weekends shall be free.'

'All right, Mr Egie, thanks.' She stood up.

'Drop the Mr Egie, Ndidi. I think we're acquainted well enough now for first names, don't you think so?'

'Eh, if you say so.'

'I do. The name is Osifo. Does it sound too awful?'

'Not at all. Thanks again, Mr Egie.' She made for the door.

'Osifo.'

'Osifo.'

You look as if you've had a sleepless night. Would you like to take the day off?' I would like to, but I've so much to do. I'm travelling to Yola tomorrow and I have to prepare for that.'

'Your assistant can do that. Take the day off. I insist. And to show that there are no hard feelings on your part about my past behaviour, let's have a game of tennis and then dinner at my place this evening. Shall I come for you at five?'

'Okay fine. I'll go home now and sleep.'

That evening, they called first at the hospital to see Eki, who was now much better, then they drove to Osifo's place. Ndidi had been there once before for an official party. He took her around the house, then they had several games of tennis and sat for pre-dinner drinks by the swimming pool. She felt happy and relaxed. She was seeing him at home for the first time on an informal occasion and he seemed an entirely different person. He wore none of the tense, anxious look he always had in the office. He laughed easily and looked attractive and full of life. She liked the house too, although it lacked the feminine touch. She wondered how deep his relationship with Itohan was, and felt a twinge of jealousy.

'I hope I didn't disrupt your plans for the evening by inviting you here. I should have asked first if you were free.'

'I'm free. I had nothing lined up.'

'Showboy not in town?'

Showboy?'

'I mean your boyfriend,  He wears such gorgeous things. A real dandy he is.'

'Oh, Gogo does love flashy clothes,' she lauded, then frowned. 'Where's my sense of loyalty? I should stand up for Gogo,' she chided herself.

'Why are you frowning?'

'I shouldn't let you take digs at my boyfriend, no matter what I think myself.'

'Another foot put wrong. I'm sorry. Let's change the topic. TeU me about yourself.'

'You tell me about yourself first. By the way, where's the girlfriend tonight?'

'Itohan? She's washing her hair or whatever it is girls do when they are not out with their boyfriends.'

'I see, proceed with your story please.'

The evening passed pleasantly enough. They discovered that they had the same taste in music and books, and had some friends in common. Osifo told her a bit about his early life with her father. She was surprised. Her father had told her that he knew Osifo slightly but had not mentioned that he had been close to his family or that he had worked for him. Osifo assured her that he had no hard feelings towards her father.

He only hoped that the Chief would improve working conditions for his workers. She promised to speak to her elder brother, Ikechukwu, who was shortly going to take over the running of their father's business. When he took her home later that night, she invited him in for a drink. He had never been inside her flat. It was simply but tastefully furnished. They listened to some music and discussed things generally. Neither of them was eager to end the evening. When she saw him to his car, he still lingered, so she had to tell him that she had not yet packed her bag for her journey the next day.

'Of course, I must not delay you. You need your beauty sleep. Good night.'

'Good night.' But still they both lingered.

'Eh, I wanted your advice on some furniture and material for curtains. My friend and his family are coming to stay with me for a week or so at the end of the month and I want to do the place up a bit. When will you be free to accompany me to the shops?'

'I don't want to.' Osifo was surprised. She had never turned down any request from him.

'May I ask why?'

'For one thing, you did not ask me nicely. You just assumed that I would come. As if it were part of my duties for the company. It isn't. Then, what will your girl say? She should do the choosing. Have you asked her?'

'No.'

'Well, do so. I wouldn't like it if Gogo sought another woman's advice about the decoration of his house. I would be terribly hurt and his explanation would have to be really good to make me want to continue with our relationship.'

He felt ashamed. No lady had ever chided him like that before. It really was not fair to Itohan.

'I suppose I didn't think. I seem to have put every foot wrong today. Thanks for shaking me up a bit. Have a nice trip. When will you be back?'

'Sunday night. I'm spending the weekend at the Yankari Game Reserve. Gogo is joining me there,'

'Lucky guy! Take care of yourself.'

I will, thanks.'

He got into his car and left.

Osifo felt a sense of loneliness at Ndidi's absence. He asked himself what was happening to him. He had never felt like this before. Each day seemed to drag into a long week. He couldn't concentrate on anything. He kept thinking of her and what she was doing. The thought that Gogo was going to join her for the weekend did not help his peace of mind. He toyed with the idea of turning up in Bauchi before Gogo did. What for? 'What's happening to me?' he asked himself again. 'I can't be in love with her! Not her of all people. I mean she's not exactly my cup of tea. For one, I don't go for light-skinned girls, not since my experience with Chichi!' She had been a lovely dark-skinned girl he had dated some years back when she was a student at the School of Basic Studies in Makurdi. Their romance had lasted exactly one term, and mostly in the form of letters.

He had driven her to the airport in Benin City one morning, kissed her tenderly and put her on her plane for Lagos, Three months later he had gone joyfully to the airport to welcome her back for the holiday and he had got a shock. He wouldn't have recognised her if she hadn't spoken. It was incredible. She had become very light-skinned, and in a sickly way too, for black patches still showed in some areas. He had had to dive into the airport bar for a quick strong drink. When asked to explain, Chichi had said that she had bleached her skin because she felt light-skinned girls appealed more to men. Osifo had made no comment. He just dropped her. Since then, he had steered clear of light-skinned girls. 'Scratch them,' he told himself, 'and you'll probably find another colour underneath.'

So, Ndidi, being light-skinned, should not be in the category of girls he fell for. He did not experience any quick heartbeats as people in love are supposed to do when they saw the object of their affection. 'Maybe I'm too old for that,' he thought. He simply enjoyed being with her. They seemed so right in each other's company. On reflection, he had to admit to himself that all those extra hours they worked at weekends was only an excuse to be with her. What did she feel about him? Not that it mattered, for dating a member of staff was out of the question for him. Perhaps if she resigned . . . Would he still feel the same way if they no longer worked together? What about Itohan? He knew then he couldn't marry her. Not while he felt the way he did about Ndidi. What was he to do?

He was surprised to note that she tried to avoid him as much as possible when she came back from her trip to the north. She was also very brief whenever she came to his office to consult him about anything. He was puzzled, but left things as they were.

One morning, when he asked for her, he was told that she had begun her annual leave. He was hurt. She should have told him that she was going away, even if only as a matter of courtesy, he told himself. He paid her a visit that evening. He was let into the flat by Eki. Ndidi was playing with the baby on the floor of the sitting room.

'Oh, Mr Egie, this is a surprise,' she said, getting up and straightening her dress. 'I hope you've not come to cut short my holiday?'

'I wouldn't dare. Not after the way you told me off the other day.'

Oh that! I was just letting off steam after a night of anxiety. You happened to be around so you were the victim. How are things going? Please sit down.'

'Thanks. You've hurt me.'

'How?'

'First of all, why Mr Egie again?'

'That was for the benefit of Eki. She might read meaning into our being on a first name basis. Why else are you hurt?'

'Why didn't you tell me that you were going away?'

'I thought you knew I was due to go on holiday this month. You approved it when I discussed it with you some weeks ago.'

'Yes, but I didn't know it would be soon. You could at least have looked in to say goodbye when you were leaving. However, that's that. Why have you been avoiding me lately?'

'What do you mean?'

'Well, you no longer stop to chat. You behave as if I've got the plague.'

'That's not right, Osifo. I only thought I shouldn't be so close. All that talk of being your "backbone" and all that.'

'You heard that, too? That was ages ago. I'm disappointed that you should allow yourself to be bothered by such silly talk.'

'I'm not really, but it might do some damage to your image in the company. I don't want that. I think you're very much your own man.'

'Thanks. That's a kind remark to make.'

'How's Itohan?'

'She's fine, thanks.'

'Where are you spending the holiday?' he asked after a while. 'Are you travelling out of the country?'

'Yes. Gogo and I are going to Nairobi and then to Europe.'

'That's nice. When are you leaving?'

'Next week.'

'Have a lovely time.'

Nairobi was fantastic and all their holiday arrangements there went without a hitch, but Ndidi did not enjoy herself as much as she had thought she would. She kept thinking of Osifo and what he was doing. Nothing Gogo did pleased her and she kept on grumbling about one thing or the other. He was perplexed and after a few days he got fed up. He had lately begun to think that their relationship was getting stale as he was beginning to feel stifled, but he was very fond of her and had thought that probably in the future they would set up home together. Now, he was having doubts. That faraway look in her eyes and her lack of attention while they were together told his experienced mind that something was brewing somewhere. Could it be another man or was she too getting stifled by their relationship? The symptoms were identical to those of Biba, his second wife, just before she ran off with an old flame of hers.

However, Gogo did not believe in allowing anything to ruin his holiday and since Ndidi was becoming a real old nag and was not enjoying herself anyway, he would have to have his holiday away from her. Perhaps when they were back in Nigeria things would improve. So, after yet another silly row during which she said she would not accompany him to Europe, he put her on a plane for Lagos and went on alone. They both knew that that was the end of the relationship, although they did not acknowledge it at the time.

Ndidi did not know whether to be glad or sad at the parting. She had been quite fond of Gogo, and had enjoyed their time together, but she knew that things could not continue the way they were. There had to be something definite. She still had three more weeks to go before the end of her holiday. She toyed with the idea of ringing up Osifo and telling him that she was cutting short her leave and coming back to work, but she decided against it. That would mean putting herself in the hollow of his palm again — as if she lived only for her job. Certainly she could not do that after all the noise she had made about overwork and unholy hours of duties. So, she spent two weeks with her parents in Lagos and one week in Benin City. She had a relaxed time doing precisely what she liked, but she missed Osifo's company badly, and kept hoping that he would call. 'What for?' she asked herself. 'As far as he's concerned I'm still another man's girl.' She was too shy to ring him up or drop by at his house. She realised that she was in love with him. The feeling had developed progressively from their first meeting,

In spite of her attempts to suppress it. How else could she explain the fact that she actually enjoyed being with him (even though it was all work) more than being with her boyfriend? She needed no persuasion to work all those extra hours. Apart from liking his physical appearance, she admired his intelligence and his purposeful way of tackling problems. Nothing seemed to baffle him for long. He always found a way. Above all, she enjoyed his company, although Gogo was a lot livelier. Gogo could entertain a girl for a whole week and still she would not be bored. He would think up all sorts of things to do and places to go to. She enjoyed these activities too, but somehow it made life seem a little bit shallow to her. Surely, there was more to life than just living it up enjoying one's self. You wouldn't catch Gogo dead worrying about a problem, particularly if it had nothing to do with his job. 'You couldn't change the world even if you tried,' he used to tell her, 'so leave it as it is, disasters and all.'

During her last week she got a phone call from her father asking her to go to Uzeri to see that their country house there was cleaned up as he was coming down shortly with some friends for a weekend. She smiled, for she knew what that meant. The crafty old man! He and his friends were no doubt bringing gifts for the chiefs and elders of the village. Later, they would visit Ute and neighbouring villages which formed part of Chief Amengo's constituency. Elections were just fifteen months away and he was taking no chances.

She liked the country house in Uzeri with its vast grounds and lovely garden. It was looked after by a couple in the village. One thing she missed while there was a tennis court. Perhaps her father could be persuaded to build one and she could come down with friends for weekends. It would help ease the boredom of a visit, for most of the time all she could do was sit in the garden and read, or go for long walks. It was while on one of these walks that she came across a sign outside a house which read 'THE EGIES'. She was curious. Could it be the same family as Osifo's? Perhaps it was a brother or a cousin? She remembered that he had once told her that their fathers had been playmates at Uzeri.

Was he an Uzeri man then, or did his family live there temporarily as hers once did? Were his parents still alive? She suddenly realised that she knew next to nothing about him, and yet he was constantly in her thoughts. She stood by the gate looking at the sign and trying to make up her mind whether to go in and ask if it was the same family as his. She had never been to that part of the village before, but she knew that the villagers were usually friendly, and wouldn't consider such a question impertinent. However, things were made easier for her when a disembodied voice said, 'How's the holiday girl?' She whirled round and almost fell into Osifo's arms. Her heart did a somersault and she blushed. 'Oh dear,' she thought, 'what will he think of me? He must think that I'm running after him, standing here and gazing at his house like an idiot.'

'I was just passing by and er . . . er . . .'

'No excuses,' he said, gazing into her eyes, his own dancing with mischief.

'Welcome to Uzeri. I didn't know you came down here.'

'This is only my second visit, and I've not been here for several years. My father's coming down next weekend with some friends and I came to make sure that everything would be ready for them.' 'Good girl. Well, you're welcome all the same. Come into our humble abode and meet my parents.'

Ndidi has calmed down now. She looked at him with curiosity. He looked so attractive in his track- suit. He must have been out jogging.

'What are you doing out here at mid-week, Osifo?'
she asked.

'Nothing. Just thought I'd take a few days off and
rest.'

'It's unlike you to leave the office and take a rest
during the week.'

'Oh well, we all change. Come in.' He led
her into a large sitting-room with old but
comfortable furniture. The walls were covered with
family photographs.

'I only arrived last night. Please sit down.' What he
did not tell her was that he had been to her flat and
had been told by a neighbour that she had travelled
to Uzeri and he had come chasing after her. What
had prompted the visit to the flat was that twice in
the last few days, he had seen Gogo in the company
of another girl. He had been surprised because
Gogo and Ndidi were usually inseparable whenever
Gogo was in town, and anyway they had gone away
together on holiday.

He decided to find out in a subtle way what had taken place. If she was free, then he would have to let her know what he felt about her, for he knew he was in love with her. Being in love he discovered, filled you with glow, but not knowing whether your love was returned was pure torture. He was determined to find out, yet he still held back. What if she rejected him later, as Madam Adunni had done? What if she laughed in his face when he pleaded how much he loved her? No, that could never happen with Ndidi. The Madam Adunni affair had been different — he was a young inexperienced boy she had picked up and later discarded. Looking back now he felt that she did not send him away out of callousness. Where could such a relationship have led? It would have ended sooner or later if the lady had been almost old enough to be his mother. What he had felt for her was initially admiration and then, later, gratitude for providing him with a home when he badly needed one. It was not love. Infatuation per¬ haps. So, in a way, she didn't actually reject his love. He realised now that he had no grounds for holding himself back from falling in love.

He looked now at Ndidi, his heart beating with love. He couldn't say why he was in love with her. He knew he always wanted her by his side. He hoped she cared too.

'What do you think of our village?' he asked her, trying to act casually.

'It's cute, but a bit too quiet. You could almost hear a pin drop. Ute is a lot livelier.'

'That's true. It's also larger.'

'How often do you come down here?'

'Almost every weekend. That is, since you stopped working with me on weekends,' he added looking straight into her eyes.

'Don't you find it boring here?' she asked, looking away. 'What do you want to do?'

'I think. It's here I come to indulge in my dreams. '

'I see.'

'Won't you ask me what my dreams are about? Aren't you curious?'

'Er . . . er . .' she stammered.

'So, did you enjoy your trip to East Africa and Europe?'

'Yes, I did. It was er . . . er . . . very nice.' 'Why not tell the truth?' she scolded herself. It would be too embarrassing, she realised.

'And the boyfriend? Did he enjoy it too?'

'Oh, yes. In fact we're planning another one for the Christmas holiday.'

'Really?' he asked, looking at her searchingly.

'Yes,' she gushed. 'That safari was simply out of this world.'

'I'm pleased you enjoyed yourselves,' he said coolly. 'Ah, here comes my father. Papa, meet

Ndidi, Chief Amengo's daughter. We are colleagues.'

'I'm glad to meet you, my daughter. You're the spitting image of your mother. It's nice to meet you at last. Our son has told us how efficient you are at your job. That's very good.'

'Thank you, sir,' said Ndidi, blushing.

'How's your father? I've not seen him for a long time. Is he well? He lives most of the time in Lagos now, I understand.'

'Yes, sir, he does. He'll be coming down here next weekend.'

'Is that so? We must invite him here for a meal. Have you met my wife?'

'No, sir.'

'I'll call Mama,' said Osifo as he left the room. Shortly, he came back with his mother, a plump, jolly woman of about sixty.

'Mama, meet Ndidi, Chief Amengo's daughter.'

'Is that who she is? Ah, you're welcome my daughter,' she greeted the girl. She went to Ndidi and embraced her.

My, you're a pretty girl. My son omitted to tell us that. He said you work like a man and that he didn't know what he would do without your support and cooperation. Thank you, my daughter.'

'Thank you, Ma. Osifo is a nice boss. We all enjoy working with him.' She flashed him a smile and he grinned.

'But he works too hard, don't you think?' asked Mrs Egie.

'I think so too, Ma. Sometimes, he doesn't know when to stop,'

'That's true. He wouldn't listen to us. I stay awake some nights worrying about him. The thought of him breaking down in health from overwork is constantly in my mind. What would I do? It would be the end of me.'

'I won't break down, Mama,' soothed Osifo. 'I come down here regularly to rest.'

'Yes, but that's only once or twice a month. And who looks after you over there? Nobody! You refused to get. .. '

'Here we go again,' put in Osifo hastily, getting up and making for the door.

'Come, Ndidi, let me show you the poultry and the fruit garden. Mama, Papa, excuse us.'

'The young lady must stay for lunch,' his mother called after them. 'I'm making Banga soup with fish and starch. Will she like that?'

'Yes, Ma,' answered Ndidi. 'Thank you.'

'I'm sorry I had to hurry you out of there just now. My mother is always at me for not getting married.'

'Well, why don't you?'

'What about you? Isn't the lover boy willing to settle down?' They looked at each other and burst out laughing.

'All right, point noted,' said Ndidi. 'Let's talk about something else. How are things going in the office? I hope Udoh has been given satisfaction?'

'Yes, he has. He's good. No problem with him at all, but we've all missed you.'

'That's very flattering. Thank you, Osifo.'

'You're welcome. By the way, there's been some development about the branch we want to open in Ibadan. We've got a place now and the fitters are at work. It should open in two months' time.'

'That would be great. We're going places.'

'I hope so. It's the assembly plant that I'm really looking forward to. When we have that, then I'll feel that we've really achieved something.'

'When will that be?'

'I don't know. Two, three years? Maybe longer. The Board is trying to raise the necessary capital. It isn't easy. However, right now, we're looking for a manager for the Ibadan Branch. We've advertised. We want a dynamic person who will be able to give us a strong foothold in the keenly competitive electronics market there.'

When she went back to work, Ndidi decided to apply for the Ibadan post. There would be no promotion for her for the position was on a par with her present one, but she felt she could do the job well, and a change of atmosphere would be welcome. After the blunder she had made in pretending that her romance with Gogo was still on, Osifo had kept his distance. He had expressed no emotion when she informed him that she had applied for the post, other than to point out that even though the job carried a lot of responsibility, he was quite sure that she would be able to cope if appointed.

It was tough at the interview and Ndidi did not think she would be appointed, but after hours of heated argument, the panel finally agreed to offer her the job. Funnily enough, after the initial surprise, her letter of appointment and the congratulatory messages from colleagues and friends failed to bring the surge of joy she had anticipated. Instead she had felt a sense of disappointment. She should be looking forward to her new and challenging job, but she wasn't. She didn't want to go to Ibadan. She wanted Osifo.

# Chapter 7

At the send-off party given her by the company some months later, she put on a bright front as she went about chatting with the guests, but how her heart ached, particularly when she saw Itohan at Osifo's side. Itohan had not been invited to the party but she had turned up anyway, much to the annoyance of Osifo, just to make sure that Ndidi was indeed leaving Benin City. She had been overjoyed at the news of the impending departure because she had lately begun to suspect that Osifo's interest in Ndidi was getting beyond that of boss/employee. She was not in love with him for she considered him dull and a workaholic but she hated being upstaged by any other female.

She took pride in the fact that she dictated the pace of her relationship with men. She wouldn't want to marry Osifo if she found a more dashing and exciting suitor, but it would be nice to keep up the relationship in order to have someone to fall back on. After all, he was quite eligible in all respects as a husband, and she knew that he was fond of her.

After the party, Ndidi went home. She had made up her mind. She didn't want the job any more. She didn't want to continue working for the company either; and neither did she want to live in Benin City. She couldn't be so near Osifo and yet know that her feelings for him were not returned as they obviously weren't. She just wanted to get lost. Perhaps she would go to her parents in Lagos or to her brother who worked in Maiduguri, and then later sort herself out. Yet again! She seemed to be doing it all the time!

She drafted her letter of resignation, typed it out and attached a cheque for one month's salary in lieu of notice. Early the next morning, she dropped the letter in Osifo's 'In' tray, and went to her office to clear out her desk. There were tears in her eyes.

'I should be happy,' she told herself, 'after all, this is the type of revenge I've always wanted to take. To let Osifo down when it would hurt and embarrass him most.' But she wasn't happy. Her heart was heavy as she thought of him. She rushed out of the office before her inquisitive colleagues arrived, and sat around listlessly all day in her flat waiting for something to happen.

She was very disappointed when there was no word from anyone in the office throughout that day. She felt unloved and unwanted. 'What did I expect? That he would come running after me? Or that the world would stand still because I've resigned my job? Am I indispensable?' She began to regret the impulse that had made her resign in the first place. It was childish and irresponsible, to say the least. She should have gone to Ibadan and begun a new life. But what about Osifo? Two agonising days later, he rang her up.

'Ndidi? What's this? I've just opened your letter. I've been away to Uzeri seeing my mother who was ill.' 'Oh, Pm sorry to hear that. I hope she's getting better.'

'Yes, she is. My presence seemed to help a lot. Now what's the resignation all about? Is it to humiliate me?'

'No, I er . . . er . . . felt I couldn't continue the way we er . . . er . . . were . . .'

'What way? Anyway, Ndidi, remain just where you are. I'm coming over. We'll sort out everything. I've something to tell you.'

'Er. . . is it necessary? Eh, Gogo is around and...' She could have kicked herself. What was she trying to say?

'Hang Gogo,' he said, 'I'm on my way.' And he hung up.

She rushed about feverishly, tidying up herself and the flat. Her heart was beating fast with anticipation. What was he coming to say? Did he love her? She didn't want him to think that her letter of resignation was a design to make him take an interest in her. That would be too cheap. That was why she had tried to tell him that Gogo was around. That bit now seemed foolish and absurd to her. What pride was she trying to protect? 'With all my claims to sophistication and women's lib, I should be able to tell a man I love him if I really do. No, I can't. It wouldn't do. The man should proclaim his love first.'

Three-quarters of an hour later, she opened the door to his ring on the bell. Inside the flat, they stood looking at each other for some seconds; he held out his arms and she rushed into them. They were both trembling slightly with emotion and held on to each other tightly for a long and passionate kiss. There was no need for words. When he released her, he led her to a settee and sat down with her.

'Ndidi,' he said gently, cupping her face in his palm, 'look at me. I love you with all my heart. Do you love me?'

'Osifo, I love you with all my heart too,' she said, and she hid her face on his shoulder. He held her close.

'My darling is shy?' he asked after a while.

'Well, yes, when it comes to admitting that I love you, I am,' she giggled nervously.

'That suits me. I like shy girls. Tell me, why don't you want to work for us any more? I'm curious.'

'Because I love you,' she said simply. 'I didn't want to leave you and go to Ibadan, and I couldn't continue working with you here feeling the way I do. The best thing was to go away. Does it make sense?'

'Darling, I don't know. Perhaps it does. Subconsciously, I've always loved you, but I kept fighting my feelings. You were so taken up with Gogo and I was jealous and so I tried to devise a way of having you alone, hence all those weekends we worked together. You must have guessed they were unnecessary.'

'But I enjoyed them.'

'Did you? You were always so distant in your attitude towards me. You can't imagine what agony I went through when you went away on holiday with that. . .'

'I was miserable too. Osifo, about Gogo and me. We have er . . . er . . . parted.'

'Have you? Well, I had my suspicions. I tried to find out that day at Uzeri. Why the pretence then?'

'I thought it was embarrassing, you found me at your gate. You might have thought that I was setting my cap at you if I had told you that Gogo and I had parted. It would have been too convenient. Moreover, I didn't know how you felt about me.'

'We've both been silly. What's wrong with letting someone know how you feel about him or her?'

'Fear of rejection perhaps.'

'Maybe. I'll tell you something that will be accepted.'

'What's that?'

'Your resignation from the company.'

'I thought I could withdraw it and go to Ibadan now that I know that you love me.'

'Not on your life! What sort of a man do you take me for? How can I live alone here while my wife lives in Ibadan? Impossible! I've waited for you all my life.'

'Oh, Osifo darling,' she said, collapsing into his arms, her eyes shining with joy,, 'it's so good to hear you say that.'

'Ndidi,' he said, holding her away from him and looking into her eyes. 'Will you marry me?'

'Yes, Osifo. I will,' she answered shyly.

Both sets of parents were pleased at the impending union. Chief Amengo, for the first time in his life, was at a loss for words to express himself when news got to him that Osifo wanted to marry his daughter. He was full of admiration for the young man who had worked very hard to get to the top. Why, it wasn't all that long ago that he had been his Assistant Supervisor in Ute. Although he had liked the flamboyant Gogo, he couldn't wish for a better husband for his beloved daughter than Osifo. He still shook with anger whenever he thought of Seju. That memory was like a bad dream.

Four months later, at the big wedding reception he gave the couple, he got up to make a speech.

'Ladies and gentlemen,' he said, 'if ever there was a marriage in which tradition permitted that the bride be given away free to the worthy bridegroom, this would have been it, for Osifo is like a son to me, as indeed his father has always been like a brother to me. This is certainly a great day in my life.'

'Hear, hear,' shouted Wale at the back of the hall. 'Osifo is tops.'

The bride blushed and the audience clapped.

While on a visit to Uzeri alone one Saturday, Osifo's mother called him aside and said, 'I'm not happy, my son.'

'Why, Mama? What's the matter?'

'You've been married almost seven months now and your wife is yet to show any sign of pregnancy. I'm very worried. Has she seen a doctor about it yet? Some wicked neighbours around here say that she might be barren and that might have been the cause of the breakdown of her first marriage.'

He laughed. He knew what gossip was like in the village and could picture what his mother must have been through. A month after any wedding, people watched out keenly for any signs of pregnancy in the bride. If these were delayed, then people would think the girl was barren.

'Em, I don't think so, Mama, although she's never discussed it with me. As a matter of fact. . .'

'Your Aunt Ebere suggested that Ndidi's probably finding it difficult to get pregnant due to the game she plays — what do you call it? That game that you both like so much; in which you dash here and there chasing a ball.'

'Tennis, Mama?'

'Yes, tennis. Now that she's married she should stop chasing that small ball around and rest the womb. I want grandchildren from her as soon as possible. I may not have long to live.'

'You do, Mama, and you know it. You're going to live to be a hundred. Anyway, why don't you speak to Ndidi? She's your daughter now. She'll listen to you. I agree with you that she should rest in the womb,' he added with a twinkle in his eyes.

'Thank you, my son. I knew you'd see it my way. I'll pay her a visit next week. Send the driver for me. I like Ndidi a lot, you know. She's nice. I'm lucky in my daughters-in-law. Ifeanyi's wife is like a daughter to me.'

'Yes, Lily is very nice.'

'Anyway, my son, if Ndidi is still not pregnant after two years, you should take another wife who can live with me here and bear you children. Ndidi wouldn't mind since she would be the recognised wife.'

'Would you like that. Mama? That I should have two wives?'

The old woman thought for a while.

'No, I wouldn't like it at all. It would be too much strain, but. . .''Shall I let you into a secret?'

'What's that?'

'Ndidi is already pregnant. That's why she hasn't been down here for some time now. She was told to rest for a while. The doctor said we should expect a set of twins.'

'Heavens be praised!' she cried excitedly, dancing. She turned to the direction of the river and raised her arms. 'Olokun, the goddess of the sea, I salute you, O. If Ndidi, my son's wife, has her baby safe and sound, I'll sacrifice a big goat to you; and if indeed it is a set of twins, then it will be two big goats. Don't let me down O!'

Osifo smiled and hugged his mother. 'I must go back now. Mama. Ndidi will be waiting anxiously. She's all alone.'

'Go in peace my son. All will be well.'